Ghostly Graveyard

by

Kathi Daley

This book is a work of fiction. Names, characters, places, and incidents either are products of the author's imagination or are used fictitiously. Any resemblance to actual events or locales or persons, living or dead, is entirely coincidental.

I want to thank the very talented Jessica Fischer for the cover art.

I so appreciate Bruce Curran, who is always ready and willing to answer my cyber questions.

And, of course, thanks to the readers and bloggers in my life, who make doing what I do possible.

Thank you to Randy Ladenheim-Gil for the editing.

Special thanks to Nancy Farris, Brandy Barber, Shirley Ericson, Joanne Kocourek, Connie Correll, and Marie Rice for submitting recipes.

And finally I want to thank my sister Christy for always lending an ear and my husband Ken for allowing me time to write by taking care of everything else.

Books by Kathi Daley

Come for the murder, stay for the romance.
Buy them on Amazon today.

Zoe Donovan Cozy Mystery:

Halloween Hijinks
The Trouble With Turkeys
Christmas Crazy
Cupid's Curse
Big Bunny Bump-off
Beach Blanket Barbie
Maui Madness
Derby Divas
Haunted Hamlet
Turkeys, Tuxes, and Tabbies
Christmas Cozy
Alaskan Alliance
Matrimony Meltdown
Soul Surrender
Heavenly Honeymoon
Hopscotch Homicide
Ghostly Graveyard
Santa Sleuth – *December 2015*

Paradise Lake Cozy Mystery:
Pumpkins in Paradise
Snowmen in Paradise
Bikinis in Paradise
Christmas in Paradise
Puppies in Paradise
Halloween in Paradise

Whales and Tails Cozy Mystery:
Romeow and Juliet
The Mad Catter
Grimm's Furry Tail
Much Ado About Felines
Legend of Tabby Hollow
Cat of Christmas Past – *November 2015*

Seacliff High Mystery:
The Secret
The Curse
The Relic
The Conspiracy
The Grudge – *December 2015*

Road to Christmas Romance:
Road to Christmas Past

Chapter 1

Friday, October 23

"Today, October 23, marks the one hundredth anniversary of the death of Isaac Wainwright," I began. I'd been asked to tell ghost stories to a group of elementary-school-aged children as part of the Haunted Hamlet activities the town of Ashton Fall sponsored each October. This was the first of three story times I'd been asked to fill over the weekend, so I decided to share a story that some believed was actually true.

"Isaac came to the area as a stranger with a mission. A mission most believe he was unable to carry out."

"What was the man's mission, Mrs. Zimmerman?" a little girl with bright blue eyes and long red hair asked. My name is actually Zoe Donovan Zimmerman now that I've married the love of my life, Zak Zimmerman, but most people still refer to me as Zoe Donovan, so I found I was momentarily thrown by the girl's question. I was half-expecting Zak's mom to walk up behind me, which, trust me, would have been a lot more horrifying than the tale I was about to tell.

"You can call me Zoe," I replied. I wasn't sure I'd ever get used to being called Mrs. Zimmerman. Not that I wasn't proud to be Zak's wife, but it sounded so formal, and I'm an informal sort of girl.

"Isaac's mission was one of the best-kept secrets around, but most believe he came to this area to find a sacred stone, although it's hard to tell where the truth ends and the legend begins," I continued.

"Like a diamond?" the girl asked.

"Perhaps. All we really know for certain is that Isaac came to Devil's Den to find something that had been hidden somewhere in the area. While no one knows for certain where the item was concealed, many believe it was stashed away in the caverns that run under and around the town."

"Devil's Den?" a young boy with dark hair and dark eyes asked. "I thought the story was about someone who died here in Ashton Falls."

I readjusted the pumpkin-stem hat I wore on my head to keep it from hanging over my eyes. "Devil's Den is what Ashton Falls used to be called when it was a mining town."

"Why'd they change the name?" the boy asked. "Devil's Den is way more awesome than Ashton Falls."

I couldn't agree more.

"The mining camp closed in 1945 and everyone moved away." I stepped behind the podium and pulled at the green tights that were threatening to give me a wedgie. "In 1955 Ashton Montgomery came here and decided to redevelop it. He named it Ashton Falls."

"What does redevelop mean?" a blond-headed girl asked.

"It means he rebuilt it and fixed it up."

"So if I find an old town and fix it up I can name it Jimmy's town?" asked the dark-haired boy, who I gathered was named Jimmy.

"I suppose."

"I want my own town," someone else said.

Every child in the place began to shout out what they would name their own town should they have one. When had I totally lost control of this presentation? These kids were going to eat me alive if I didn't do something fast. I stepped out from behind the podium and tried to make my five-foot frame, which was dressed like a jack-o'-lantern, look taller and threatening.

I clapped my hands and asked everyone to settle down.

"Perhaps we should save the questions and comments until the end," I suggested.

The room quieted down after a few minutes.

"As I was saying," I continued, "Isaac Wainwright came to Devil's Den to find a sacred stone."

"Why was it sacred?" the redheaded girl asked.

"It was purported to have special powers."

"Could it make you fly?" a tall, thin boy asked.

"No, I don't think it could make you fly."

"If I had a magic rock I would want it to be able to make me fly."

"The stone was sacred, but I don't know if it was magic," I answered.

"Was it real?" a petite blond-headed girl from two rows back asked.

"Yes, the stone was real. Or at least the legend tells of a stone that was real. I'm not really sure at this point. Like I said, it's hard to tell where the truth ends and the legend begins."

"My dad got my mom a ring for their anniversary, but she got mad 'cause it wasn't real."

I took a deep breath and prayed for patience. Normally I was good with kids, but these were kicking my butt. Maybe it was the tights and fuzzy pumpkin face around my middle. I looked like a pregnant Peter Pan.

"Anyway, as I was saying, Isaac came to the area to look for the stone, but on a dark and moonless night, not long after he arrived, his headless body was found in the old Devil's Den cemetery."

"Cool," several voices from the crowd murmured.

"It's said that on the hundredth anniversary of his death he will rise from the grave to enact his revenge on the man who killed him."

"Wouldn't the man who killed him already be dead?" asked a much-too-logical-for-a-ghost-story boy, who looked to be in the fifth or sixth grade.

"Yes, I imagine he would be. I guess maybe he'll have to take his revenge out on his killer's descendants."

"What's a descendant?" one of the girls in the front row asked.

"It's someone who comes in your family after you. Like a child or grandchild."

One of the younger girls in the crowd began to cry.

"What's wrong?" I asked.

"I don't want Isaac to enact his revenge on me."

I got down off the stage of the auditorium and hurried to where the girl was sitting. I bent down so that we were eye to eye, although my big pumpkin belly prevented me from hugging her. "Oh, no. You don't have to worry. It's just a spooky story for Halloween. It's not real."

"I thought in the beginning you said your story was based on an actual legend," the logical sixth grader said.

"Yeah, I did say that, didn't I?"

"Did you lie? 'Cause if you did, you shouldn't lie to kids."

"No," I defended myself, "I didn't lie. Exactly. I just embellished the truth to make the story scarier." I turned to look at the little girl who was still crying. "But I promise, no one is going to die. You're perfectly safe. It's just a story."

I looked around the auditorium full of kids. Some looked bored; others looked terrified. Whose idea was this anyway? If the events committee was going to tell scary stories shouldn't the kids be segregated by age? Maybe I'd bring it up at the next meeting.

"So who wants punch and cookies?" I asked.

Thank God Zak had thought to have me bring a snack. I should have let him tell the story. He had a way with kids that apparently I did not. Maybe I'd give away my other story times and volunteer for something like gravedigger or door monitor. Something safe, where I wouldn't have to worry about traumatizing little girls or outsmarting much-too-smart preteen boys.

"So how did it go?" my best friend, Ellie Davis, asked when the story time had concluded and the sugared-up kids had been returned to their parents. I'd changed back into my jeans and sweatshirt and felt like my old self again.

"Horrible. Worse than horrible."

"What's worse than horrible?" Ellie asked.

"A word isn't coming to mind, but believe me, my story time was a disaster. I should have brought Charlie. Kids love Charlie, but I wasn't sure I'd have time to take him home between events so I left him with Bella and Digger."

Charlie is my dog, Bella is Zak's dog, and Digger is our ten-year-old ward Scooter's dog.

"How did you do with the dunk tank?" I asked.

Ellie reached up and grabbed a chunk of her still-wet hair. "Let me tell you, agreeing to be dropped from a ledge into a tub of freezing cold water is not the sort of thing any sane and rational adult should agree to do. Why did we ever think it was a good idea to have a dunk tank anyway?"

"It seems like the dunk tank and the story time both came from the same source," I reminded Ellie.

"Duncan."

Duncan Wright was the newest member of the events committee. He'd moved to Ashton Falls less than a month ago but was already establishing himself as a mover and shaker. He'd joined our little group and in less than an hour changed half the plans I'd spent months coming up with for this year's Hamlet.

"I was supposed to work at the ticket booth, but Leroy didn't show, so I got stuck being the sucker who ended up in the water. At least I had a change of clothes in my car," Ellie commented. "I really didn't have time to go home before heading over to the pumpkin patch. What's up next for you?"

"I'm heading over to the kiddie carnival to sell tickets for the games, and then I have the ghostly graveyard and haunted house tonight."

"Oh, good. I have the graveyard tonight as well. I think Levi does too. Will Zak be there?"

"Hopefully. He had to fly out this morning to meet with a client, but he assured me he would be home in time to help out with the haunted house."

"That new customer still giving him problems?" Ellie asked.

"Yeah. But he says he has it handled. Pi went with him. Maybe between the two of them they can get everything programed the way the man wants once and for all."

Pi, aka Peter Irwin, is one of three minors Zak and I have taken under our wings. He's a sixteen-year-old computer genius who attends the local high school for half the day and Zimmerman Academy, the private school Zak and I have established for gifted kids, the other half. After his mother died and he was put into foster care he'd gotten himself into quite a bit of trouble, but he seemed to be doing much better now that he was with us.

"Alex is helping Phyllis and the girls at the snack bar, but she wanted to help me at the pumpkin patch if it's okay with you," Ellie informed me.

Alex is the third minor in our care, a ten-year-old genius who's much more mature than a ten-year-old should be.

"Whatever she wants to do is fine," I answered. "Both Alex and Scooter are spending the night at my parents. I wasn't sure what time Zak and I would get home and I didn't know Pi's plans. My dad is going to pick them up whenever I text him."

"Okay, then I guess I'll head over and pick up Alex and see you at the graveyard later. Don't let them talk you into helping with the tank," Ellie warned. "It's brutal."

While I had no intention of volunteering for the dunk tank I was certain it couldn't be any more brutal than story time. Although I was brought up an only child and hadn't had a lot of experience with children prior to the past year, I take my role as guardian to Scooter, Alex, and Pi quite seriously and am beginning to think of myself as someone who's competent to deal with the preadult population of Ashton Falls. Not only did I provide parenting for Alex and Scooter, and to Pi, to some degree, on a daily basis, but I was room mom for Scooter's class and a PTA board member at his school. I also help out as snack mom for soccer and assistant parent helper for the play Alex is starring in. Now, after my simply horrific afternoon, I'd lost all the kid confidence I'd thought I was starting to build.

The truth of the matter was, Zak was much better at this parenting thing than me. He seemed to have a natural knack with kids, while I'm much more comfortable with kids of the four-legged variety. When I'm at the Zoo, the wild and domestic rescue and rehabilitation shelter I own and operate, I feel confident and in control. I can stare down a bear or train even the most difficult dog, but apparently I'm quite helpless against a sixth grader with an attitude.

The kiddie carnival was in full swing by the time I arrived. Although I came into the month as chairperson of the Haunted Hamlet, it seemed as if Duncan had taken over since he'd arrived in town. It wasn't that I minded sharing the work and responsibility—in fact, I hadn't wanted to be chairperson in the first place—but I did mind the fact that he seemed to have taken over after I'd already done most of the work.

"I'm glad you're here," Duncan greeted me when I arrived. "I need you to head over to the pie toss."

"The pie toss? I thought I was supposed to supervise the booths and sell tickets this afternoon."

"I can do that. I really need you to fill in for Leroy. I guess he's sick, or he had some sort of family emergency or something. I'm not quite clear on the details, but I know he isn't here."

Lucky Leroy.

"Okay, so what do you need me to do at the pie toss? Sell tickets?"

"No. We need you to provide the target."

"The target?" My heart sank.

"Yeah, you know; I need you to stand behind the plywood form and let the kids throw pies at your face."

I let out a long breath. "You know I'm a good sport, but I have to be at the graveyard in a couple of hours and I'll probably be there a good part of the night. I won't have time to go home and shower and change between the pie toss and the graveyard, which will make for a sticky and uncomfortable evening. Isn't there someone else who can do it?"

Duncan frowned at me. "I thought you were a team player."

"I am a team player. Ask anyone. But maybe the pie toss would be better served with one of the kids as a target. Kids like to do things like that. Or even an adult who doesn't have other obligations afterward. Maybe someone like you?"

Duncan swatted me on the butt. "Sorry, kid; I've got plans later, so I guess you're up."

"I'm not a kid and I don't appreciate the slap on the butt," I replied.

"Don't be such a whiner," Duncan instructed. "You signed up to help, so help. I'm a busy man and I don't have time to babysit complainers like you. Now either get your perky little backside over to the pie toss or go home. I have a Hamlet to run."

I wanted to scream. I actually wanted to throw myself onto the ground and kick and scream, but that would only have lent legitimacy to his kid comment.

"What was that all about?" my good friend Levi Denton asked after Duncan walked away.

Levi is the third member of the Zoe-Ellie-Levi triad. We'd been best friends since kindergarten and I predicted we'd still be best friends when we were old and gray.

"Did you hear what he said?" I asked.

"Part of it," Levi admitted.

"The nerve of the guy," I shouted, louder than was socially appropriate. "He shows up in *my* town and joins *my* committee and then walks right into *my* event and takes over *my* job. The man needs to be brought down a peg. No one talks to Zoe Donovan Zimmerman that way and lives to tell about it."

Levi took my arm and pulled me to the side. "Maybe you should bring it down a notch."

I looked around. There were a couple of dozen people staring at me.

"Yeah, I guess maybe I should." I took a deep breath and took a step away.

"Where are you headed?" Levi asked.

"To have a pie or maybe a couple dozen pies thrown in my face."

"I'll cover for you at the graveyard if you want to run home and take a shower when you're done," Levi offered.

"Thanks. I'll take you up on that."

I walked down Main Street toward the park where the pie toss was set up. The more I thought about the way Duncan was steamrolling everyone the madder I got. He was new in town. If he wanted to help out he should take a backseat to those of us with more experience with this event. I was the chairperson, so I should be the one making the decisions. Besides, I really didn't want to get pies tossed in my face. Maybe I could just buy all the pies so there wouldn't be any to toss at me. The committee would get their money and I would avoid whipped cream up the nose. I smiled. There were times having a rich husband came in handy.

Of course as luck would have it, there was a long line of snot-nosed adolescents waiting who weren't at all supportive of my plan. I put the rubber apron around my body and took my position behind the barrier. I glared at the first sixth grader as he lifted his pie plate into the air.

"I'll give you twenty dollars to miss," I tried.

The kid smiled an evil little grin and let the plate fly.

I closed my eyes and prayed the pie would land harmlessly on the ground in front of me.

It didn't.

The next kid in line couldn't be more than five. I doubted she would be able to do the damage the older child had been able to inflict. I actually began to relax when pie number two hit me smack dab in the middle of the face.

I cleared the whipped cream from my eyes and looked toward the sound of deep laughter. I couldn't help but notice the very satisfied glance Duncan Wright sent in my direction. There was no doubt about it: The man had set me up, and before the night was over Zoe Donovan was going to enact her revenge.

Chapter 2

It was a perfect night for the kickoff of the Haunted Hamlet festivities. The air was calm and moderately warm considering the time of year. The golden leaves that hung from the aspen trees glistened as they reflected off the white twinkle lights we'd strung everywhere. This year the haunted house was to be held in an abandoned building just outside of town. The deserted residence we'd chosen to use for the event was located next to the old Devil's Den cemetery.

The cemetery hadn't been used in almost a century. After Ashton Montgomery redeveloped the area, he'd built a new cemetery up on the hill, and the land where the miners and their families were buried had fallen into a state of decay. A lot of the tombstones were still there, but many of the markers, which consisted of little more than two sticks nailed together, had long since vanished.

Our plan for the event was to have parking in the vacant field on the far side of the cemetery. Visitors would then be led by the "ghost" of Isaac Wainwright through the cemetery toward the house, which had been decorated to frighten even the bravest souls among us. The haunted house was an event that was designed to appeal to older teens and adults, so the first tours hadn't been scheduled until after dark, giving the atmosphere an extraspooky feel.

"Boo!" someone shouted behind me.

I jumped and screamed as I stepped out of my car.

"You almost gave me a heart attack," I complained to Levi.

"It's Halloween. You should expect to be scared."

"Maybe in the house or even in the graveyard, but not in the parking lot. Where's Ellie?"

"She's not going to make it," Levi told me.

I frowned. "Really? I just spoke to her this afternoon and she said she was going to show after she finished at the pumpkin patch."

"She got a call and had to go out of town at the last minute."

"What happened?"

"Do you remember her cousin Skye?"

"Vaguely." Skye was Ellie's mother's sister's daughter. She was a couple of years older than Ellie and the two weren't supercloser, but Skye had visited Ashton Falls a few times when we were growing up.

"Well, she was in a car accident. A bad one."

"Oh, no. Is she going to be okay?"

"Ellie said they really don't know. Skye is stable but still unconscious. I guess at this point it could go either way."

Poor Ellie. Skye lived in a small town about four hours away from Ashton Falls. Ellie was most likely still on the road if she was headed to the hospital. I knew Skye's parents had both passed during the last couple of years, so even though Ellie hadn't seen Skye in a while, I suppose she might be her closest relative next to Ellie's mom, Rosie.

"Did Ellie share her plans?" I asked.

"She was going to pick up the baby and then head back."

"The baby?"

"Apparently Skye had a baby since Ellie last spoke to her. Skye's roommate called to ask Ellie if she could keep the baby until Skye recovers. Ellie said she didn't even know the baby existed, but of course she was happy to help out."

I watched as a dark cloud moved across the moon, casting the parking area into darkness. I felt like the cloud had appeared in the clear sky as some sort of an omen. But then again, it could just have drifted in over the summit when I wasn't looking.

"How old is the baby?" I wondered.

"Six months. According to the roommate the father is a drifter Skye hadn't spoken to since the night Mariah was conceived. He's totally out of the picture, and as far as Ellie could tell, Skye hadn't maintained contact with her extended family after her parents passed."

I felt a sadness surround me. "I hope Skye is okay. I only met her a couple of times, but I remember her being a nice girl. And the poor baby. Babies need their mamas."

"Yeah." Levi sighed. "It really is a bad situation. Did Zak make it back?"

I closed my door and opened the trunk of the small car Zak had bought me to tool around town in. I began to sort through the pile of objects I'd begun carrying around since I'd become a mom of sorts.

"Yeah, he's back," I answered as I began to gather the things I would need for the evening. "Pi is going to hang out with Jeremy after he finishes his shift at the Zoo, so Zak was going to drop him off with him and then head home to check on the animals and make sure Scooter and Alex were settled at my parents'. He should be here before long."

I smiled as I found the pair of cleats Scooter had sworn someone must have stolen because he was unable to find them. I really did need to clean out my trunk. I slung my backpack over my shoulder and began to walk across the parking lot toward the trail that led from the parking lot and through the graveyard to the house.

"Fair warning," Levi said as he fell in next to me. "I really didn't want to be the one to tell you this, and was waiting until the last possible moment to do so, but someone broke in and trashed the place."

"What? Who would do such a thing?"

"Benny said he saw Duncan here earlier, so my money is on him being the culprit."

I stopped walking and looked directly at Levi. "Why would Duncan trash the place?"

"I don't know. When I arrived and saw the mess I asked Benny what happened and he said he didn't know for sure, but he'd been here earlier to check on the sound system and Duncan showed up while he was here. He said he left shortly after Duncan arrived because he needed to do some things before he came back for the evening, and Duncan agreed to lock up. My guess is either Duncan did the trashing or he forgot to lock up and vandals took advantage of that fact."

"Maybe someone broke in after Duncan left," I said.

"Maybe," Levi acknowledged. "But even if that's true he left the door open. I looked around. There's no sign of a forced entry."

I looked toward the house. The haunted house and haunted graveyard were my babies. I'd been working on them for months. I couldn't believe someone would trash the place after all my hard work.

"How bad is it?" I asked.

"Bad."

I let out a long breath and shook my head. I couldn't believe Duncan would do such a thing, but my intuition told me that he had. I felt myself getting madder and madder as I walked toward the house. What could the man who seemed to have made it his mission to annoy and irritate me possibly hope to gain by destroying the event I'd spent weeks working on? Maybe it wasn't as bad as Levi indicated.

Once I stepped inside I realized Levi hadn't been exaggerating at all. The place looked like a war zone. There were some props lying on the floor, while others had been broken beyond repair. It looked like someone had taken a baseball bat to the place. And the worst part was that someone had spread red paint all over one wall and part of the floor. It was going to take a miracle to get it out of the area rug that was on the floor in the center of the room.

"There's paint in the kitchen as well," Levi informed me.

"Great."

"I'm going to go see if I can round up some more help," Levi said.

"What happened?" Sue Stone, one of the mothers from Scooter's soccer team, asked as she came in through the door behind me after Levi had walked away.

"I really have no idea. It looks like someone intentionally trashed the place."

"Who would do such a thing?" Sue asked.

"Benny said he saw Duncan here earlier, which led Levi to suspect Duncan was our vandal, but I don't see how he could be because he was at the kiddie carnival selling tickets all afternoon."

"No," Sue corrected, "*I* spent the afternoon at the kiddie carnival selling tickets. Someone was supposed to relieve me, but no one ever showed, so I did a double shift."

I frowned. "That's odd. I was supposed to relieve you, but I ran into Duncan, who sent me to the pie toss. He said he was going to cover the ticket booth."

"Well, he didn't," Sue confirmed.

It was beginning to sound like Duncan was the culprit after all. But why would he spend hours volunteering with the events committee and then intentionally destroy any chance we had of making a profit?

"It looks like a line is beginning to form out front. We should probably tell everyone they'll need to come back tomorrow," Sue suggested. "I hate to spread the word that the house has been vandalized, though. I'm afraid that might open a whole can of worms. Maybe we can tell everyone we had a problem with the electricity. This is an old house. Most folks will buy it."

"That sounds like a good idea. Why don't you go break the news to the people in line and I'll start cleaning up?"

Luckily, we had a fairly large staff lined up to man the event that evening and most were happy to stay to clean up when they found out the event was canceled. I wasn't thrilled by what had occurred, but it looked like it was going to be possible to put everything back the way it had been so we would be able to resume operations the following evening.

"Hey, Bruce, can you oversee the graveyard tomorrow night?" I asked one of the helpers who had finished what he'd been assigned to do and was getting ready to leave.

"I thought you had someone for tomorrow."

"I did, but the *someone* I had was Duncan, and because I'm going to kill him once I track him down, I figure I'll need to replace the shift."

Bruce laughed. "I hear ya. I'll be happy to fill in."

I looked around the room. It seemed we would be finished in half the time I'd originally estimated it would take us.

"Ellie called," Levi informed me after Bruce left. "She's on her way home with the baby and wanted me to stop to pick up some stuff."

"Did she say how Skye was doing?" I asked.

"The same. Ellie is pretty worried. She said it really doesn't look good."

"Is there anything Zak and I can do?"

"Actually, there is something Zak can do. I guess your mom is going to lend Ellie an extra crib she has, and she said she had a stroller and a couple of other things as well. I don't think it will all fit in my 4Runner, but maybe if Zak could follow me in his truck…"

"No problem. I'm sure he'd be happy to help. Is there anything else we can do?"

"Not really. At least not at this point. Once she gets home we'll have some things to figure out, but it seems like for now she just really wants to get the baby settled into the boathouse."

"Of course. You and Zak go on ahead. I can finish up here. And don't worry about tomorrow. I'll find someone to cover for both you and Ellie."

"Thanks. That would help."

"And please call if you think of anything at all you need."

"I will."

I watched Levi walk across the room to speak to Zak. I couldn't help but wonder at the fate of the baby should her mother not recover. It was such a tragic thing to have occurred. It made my irritation with Duncan somehow seem petty and unimportant.

"Is there anything else I can do?" Sue asked when Levi and Zak had left.

"No, I think we're good. As soon as the guys finish fixing the sound system, I'm going to do a walk-through and then lock up for the night. Thanks again for all your help. The cleanup went a lot faster than I thought it would. As long as we can keep Duncan out of the place we should be good to open tomorrow."

"It really is a shame. I'm willing to bet the revenue from tonight's haunted house would have been the largest of the weekend, with it being opening night and all."

Sue had a point. Opening night was always the biggest one.

"It does seem like Duncan is intentionally trying to sabotage things."

"What do you really know about this guy?" Sue asked. "I heard some of the others talking about him, so I know he's new in town and that he jumped right in and took over at the events committee meetings."

"Honestly, I don't know a whole lot," I answered. "The guy showed up at a meeting three weeks ago and said he wanted to be involved. He told the committee he had a lot of experience organizing events and wanted to put his knowledge to work to help out his new hometown. He seemed sincere, and although the plans for the Hamlet were pretty much set by that point, he offered a few suggestions that seemed to make sense. Initially, he seemed to be a team player who was only trying to help, and his initial suggestions were really minor alterations that could easily be accommodated, so we ended up voting to incorporate a few of his ideas into our plans."

"So I'm going to go ahead and speculate that once he got a foot in the door he dug in and took over entirely."

"Pretty much." I nodded. "He was actually pretty sneaky about it. He started out small and then made bigger and bigger changes. Most of the things, like the story time and the addition of several games like the pie-throwing contest were discussed and voted on. A few others like the addition of the dunk tank he introduced without anyone knowing what he was doing until he did it."

Sue frowned. "What I don't get is why he went to all that trouble. He must be busy getting settled into a new job and a new home. Why would he decide to get so involved in a fund-raiser that was just around the corner?"

"Good question." The whole thing seemed odd. Too odd. My Zodar was beginning to hum and I didn't like it one bit.

"What did you say Duncan does for a living?" Sue asked.

I hesitated. "I'm not sure he ever said. If he did I don't remember what he told us."

"And where is he from?"

"No idea," I admitted. "Now that I think about it, I don't know anything about the guy other than that he's new to town and he claimed to have experience with event planning." I frowned. "Maybe Willa knows."

Willa Walton worked for the county and served as the chairperson of the events committee.

"I guess I should get going," Sue said. "If I know my family, and I do, they're all waiting for me to come home and tuck them in. I'll see you tomorrow."

"'Bye, Sue."

I looked around the room. The crew I'd called in had done an excellent job. You couldn't even tell that Duncan the destroyer had ever been here. Sue had made some good points about Duncan's past and present. What exactly did we know about him? Where was he from? Where did he live? Where did he work?

"We're all done here," Benny informed me after Sue walked away. "The others have all gone, but I wanted to check with you before I took off."

"I think we're good. I'm going to lock up and leave myself. I really want to thank you for spending the whole evening putting everything back together. I can't imagine why Duncan did this."

"The man's a bad seed. Gotta keep an eye on folks like him."

"Yes, I can see that. See you tomorrow?"

"I'll be here."

After Benny left I headed upstairs to check the top floor and make sure all the lights were turned off. The haunted house really was spooky when you were alone, even if the lights were on. I couldn't help but wonder what species of visitor was creating all the rustling sounds I could hear now that everyone had gone. I hoped it was squirrels. Or raccoons. I hated to let my imagination take over at this point, so I systematically turned off the lights and then headed back downstairs.

I found myself wishing I'd brought a flashlight. Walking back through the graveyard now that everyone was gone was going to be a hair-raising experience. I was pretty sure I'd seen a flashlight in the kitchen, so I decided to try to find it before I left. The kitchen wasn't really decorated like the main part of the building. I'd strung a few cobwebs and there were jack-o'-lanterns on the counter for effect, but I figured the crew who worked there might want to use it for breaks, so I hadn't included it as part of the tour.

I made sure the back door was locked and the back window closed. I closed the cabinets that had been left open and picked up the set of butcher's knives someone had knocked to the floor. I looked around for a large cleaver I knew was part of the set but didn't see it anywhere. I'd used it earlier to cut a piece of rope, so it was possible someone else had used it for a similar purpose and then forgotten to put it back. I looked around one more time, turned off the kitchen light, and then headed out the door.

I had to walk slowly through the dark cemetery so I wouldn't trip because I hadn't found a flashlight. Off in the distance, my car was standing alone in the parking field.

I was halfway to it when I heard a scurrying that sounded like something larger than a squirrel.

I stopped walking. "Is anyone there?"

I listened, but there was no reply. I turned and looked around the area and didn't see anything. I had taken a step closer to the car when I heard the scurrying again. I paused. The sound stopped, but I noticed a dark shape at the edge of the graveyard. I slowly left the path and started toward that shape. It was large. Maybe a bear. It was hard to make out the shape in the dark night. It seemed the cloud that had covered the moon earlier had returned and brought its friends. I stopped to listen. The air around me seemed to freeze in the silence.

I had just turned to head back to the car when I saw a movement out of the corner of my eye. I swung around only to look into the hollow eyes of a figure dressed all in black with a hood covering its face. I screamed and ran, but I didn't make it far before I tripped over something. I rolled onto my back and was preparing to fight for my life, but the figure was gone.

My heart was pounding in my chest as I sat up and tried to make out what it was I had tripped over. I had to suppress a scream when I realized it was the bloody body of Duncan Wright. And it looked like I'd found the missing kitchen cleaver.

Chapter 3

Saturday, October 24

Note to self: It isn't a good idea to plan to get an early start to the morning following a late night of being interrogated by a wet-behind-the-ears deputy when the sheriff is out of town.

Zak groaned as he rolled over and turned off the alarm.

"It feels like we just got to sleep." I yawned.

"We did just get to sleep."

"I can't believe that rookie was actually going to book me."

I was still angry about the way things had turned out. When I'd found Duncan's body I'd called Salinger, only to find out that he was on vacation and a guy from the county seat was in town to fill in. Initially, I was annoyed but not alarmed, until I found out that Deputy Warren Lesserman was an idiot. Not only had he not been helpful in the least as to helping me identify the real killer but he'd had the nerve to suggest that I'd done it.

Talk about rude.

"He's just young and wants to cover all his bases. After the tirade you left on Salinger's cell I'm sure he'll call Lesserman and get everything cleared up. In the meantime I suggest we just keep a low profile."

"Humph," I answered irritably.

Zak rolled over and pulled me into his arms. He kissed my neck. "I'm sorry this has been so rough on you, and I'm sorry Lesserman kept us up most of the night, but let's try not to let it ruin our day."

I yawned. "Yeah, you're right. I am looking forward to Scooter's game. I just don't understand why it was scheduled so early."

"It's a tournament," Zak explained. "There are games going on from dawn to dark and we just happened to be scheduled first. I'll go down and make the coffee while you catch a hot shower. You'll feel better once we get up and going."

Zak rolled away from me. I immediately wanted to pull him back, but I supposed we really didn't have time for that.

"I'll make sure the kids are up," Zak added. "I have a breakfast casserole in the freezer. I'll toss it in the microwave and it'll be ready by the time you come down."

"With biscuits?" I asked hopefully.

Zak leaned over and kissed me on the lips. "With biscuits."

I rolled myself out of bed as Zak left to get breakfast on the table. I'd tried to reason with the deputy the previous evening, but he hadn't been listening to anything I said. I mean really. If I'd killed the guy why on earth would I be the one to call it in? And yes, I knew they would find my fingerprints on the murder weapon because I'd used the cleaver to cut the rope earlier in the evening, which is why I took the initiative to explain why he would likely find them on it. The man had the nerve to call my explanation contrived.

Seriously?

After an arduous interview that seemed to go on forever, the man finally let me go, but only after warning me not to leave town. Where else would I be when there was a murder to solve? The guy had no idea who he was dealing with, but once I managed to clear the cobwebs from my brain I planned to make sure he found out.

The main problem I needed to overcome was that the substitute deputy wasn't buying my story about a man in a dark cloak. He was dressed sort of like a monk, with a robe and a large hood that concealed his face. Lesserman initially suggested I had an overactive imagination and had been seeing things that didn't actually exist. He'd then suggested that perhaps I had seen a bear. As the interview progressed he'd had the audacity to suggest that I'd made up the story of the man in the cloak to cover up the fact that it was actually me who had killed a man I'd spent a good part of the day threatening.

Don't get me wrong: I get the fact that a man in a dark cloak lurking around a cemetery on an overcast night just before Halloween sounds like something from a horror movie, but I know what I saw and it wasn't a bear.

After drying my hair I dressed in a pair of jeans, a long-sleeved T-shirt, and a harvest gold sweatshirt. Then I slipped on my winter socks and light boots. It promised to be a nice day, but at the crack of freaking dawn there was still frost on the ground.

"That smells wonderful." I took in an appreciative breath as I entered the kitchen. The rest of the family was chatting and eating Zak's delicious breakfast.

"It's really good," Alex verified as Zak set a plateful of food on the table in front of the chair where I normally sat. "There are two kinds of sausage in it. It's spicy. I like it."

"Are you ready for the big game?" I asked Scooter after taking a sip of coffee.

"I'm ready. There are twelve teams in the tournament, but I think with me and Tucker we can win."

"I'm sure you can. You've both been doing so well this season."

"Can we go into town to play some games when the soccer game is over?" Scooter asked.

I wanted to say no. I wanted to say I was going to come home and go back to bed.

"Yeah, can we?" Alex seconded.

"Absolutely." I forced a smile.

I ate my meal in silence while Zak and the kids went upstairs to finish getting ready. By the time I'd finished my third cup of coffee I was feeling a little more human. Yes, it was early, but the sun was peeking over the distant summit, which at least made it feel like it wasn't still the middle of the night. There's something about getting up when it's still dark that tends to throw my system out of whack.

"Pass the ball, pass the ball," I yelled at the top of my lungs as Scooter flew down the field toward the goal. One of his teammates was standing right in front of the goal, if he'd just pass it off as we were trying to teach him to do. Scooter was an excellent athlete, but he still needed to work on his approach to team strategy.

Scooter passed the ball to his teammate, who made the goal. And not any goal but the winning goal.

"That's my boy!" I jumped up and down, shouting. I turned and hugged Alex, who was jumping up and down as well.

"Did you see that?" Alex wrapped her arms around me. "It was an amazing play."

"Yeah," I agreed as I took a step back. "It really was."

I looked across the field, where Zak had hoisted both Scooter and his teammate up onto his shoulders as their teammates congratulated them. Zak wasn't Scooter's regular coach, but they'd been short one for the tournament so he'd agreed to fill in.

"Go find Pi," I instructed Alex. "I have to get into town early today to help out with the pumpkin carving, so we'll need to go as soon as the team finishes up."

"He's talking to one of the kids from the high school," Alex informed me as she pointed to the far end of the field. "His name is Trip. At least that's what everyone calls him. You might want to keep an eye on that one."

I frowned. "Why?"

"Brooklyn told me that Pi first made friends with him because he's involved in a band and Pi is interested in music. But she also said he has a reputation for getting into trouble. As far as she knew it was petty-crime stuff like truancy and shoplifting, but Brooklyn didn't think the guy was going to be the best influence on Pi. She said she also heard he was into recreational drugs and might have a drinking problem."

Brooklyn was one of the kids who attended Zimmerman Academy, a confident sixteen-year-old who had gotten into her own kind of trouble prior to coming to Ashton Falls. Chances were if Brooklyn thought the guy was bad news, he was. I kind of think Pi and Brooklyn might have a flirtation going on, but so far I hadn't gathered any evidence to support or disclaim my theory.

"I'll mention it to Zak," I promised. "I know Pi plans to fill in with Jeremy's band for the concert in the park tomorrow and they're practicing later this afternoon, so I think he'll be fine for today. Right now why don't you just run over and tell Pi that we're leaving?"

"Okay," Alex agreed.

"I guess you heard about the haunted graveyard." Tawny Upton walked up beside me after Alex had gone to talk to Pi. Tawny owns the Over the Rainbow Preschool and is a member of the Ashton Falls Events Committee.

"Yeah. It's a shame to cancel it after we worked so hard to get it decorated, not to mention cleaning it up yesterday."

"It's going to hurt our bottom line, that's for certain," Tawny said. "But I guess it's a crime scene with Duncan being dead and all."

"I hate to think unkindly of the dead, but being murdered in the cemetery seems like such a Duncan thing to do. I mean, really. It's as if he set out to ruin the event, and although he didn't quite manage to do it while he was alive, he pulled it off from the grave."

Tawny looked at me oddly. "You might want to refrain from saying things like that. I know you disliked the guy, but he's dead. The deputy who's covering for Salinger is going around town asking everyone if we felt you might have had motive to kill Duncan, and if you continue to bad-mouth him it's going to get back to Lesserman."

I took a deep breath. "You're right. It is uncouth of me to trash the guy when he can no longer speak for himself. I really didn't care for Duncan, but I'm sorry he was murdered. And not just because he ruined the event. I plan to try to help track down the real killer, which, in spite of my outbursts, wasn't me. Any ideas?"

Tawny thought about it. "I did hear that Willa was concerned that Duncan had gone forward with the dunk tank without taking insurance considerations into account. She mentioned that the tank provided an injury risk to the person being dunked, and the insurance rider for the specific event was going to cost more than the activity was likely to make. She was pretty mad, but I don't see her killing him over it. Still, there was something odd about the whole situation."

"Do you know anything about the guy?" I asked. "Where he lived before he moved here? What sort of job he had? Where he lived now?"

"No," Tawny answered, "though I'm sure he must have told us all of that when he showed up for his first events committee meeting."

"I don't think he did. I think he just said he was new in town and had a lot of experience with event planning and wanted to get involved. Then he tossed out a couple of good ideas for the Hamlet and before we knew it, he was not only part of the group but he'd taken over completely."

Tawny frowned. "I wonder if his enthusiasm for the event was just a ruse. Maybe he intentionally joined the committee and volunteered to help so he would have access to the venues. Maybe he planned to rob us. Or maybe he wanted to ruin the event to get revenge on someone."

"Yeah, but who and why?" I wondered.

"I don't suppose we'll ever find out now that he's dead and therefore unavailable for questioning."

After the game Pi went off to hang out with friends until it was time for him to meet up with Jeremy, and Zak took Alex and Scooter into town to play games. I headed over to the pumpkin patch, where I was scheduled to serve as cashier for a two-hour shift. When I got there I found out Hazel Hampton had been scheduled for the same shift, so I took advantage of the break to head over to the boathouse to check on Ellie and the baby.

Before I moved in with Zak I had lived in the boathouse my entire adult life. My grandfather still owns the property and I have a huge soft spot for the converted building I designed and decorated.

It had warmed up quite a lot since we'd left home, so I stopped by the house to change into lighter clothing and check on the animals. I decided to walk down the beach to the boathouse, which is just a hop, a skip, and a jump from the mansion where I now live.

It had turned out to be a beautiful autumn day. The sky was as blue as the lake, and the aspens that were sprinkled over the mountainside were a brilliant yellow and orange. The three dogs trotted along beside me. I figured I'd need to walk back to the house Zak and I share with the kids to get my car later, so I might as well get the dogs some exercise while I was out and about.

When I arrived at the boathouse Ellie was sitting on the back deck, which overlooks the water. There was a stroller beside her that was covered, but I was willing to bet the baby was asleep inside it.

Ellie's dog Shep ran out to greet his doggy friends when we arrived. I pulled up another chair and sat down next to my friend.

"You look exhausted," I commented.

"I feel exhausted. Poor Mariah doesn't know me from Adam and she's having a hard time adjusting to not having her mommy here. She cried during half of the ride home and for most of the night. She's sleeping now. She seems to like it out here."

"It's peaceful with the sound of the water lapping onto the sand, combined with the birds singing from the trees. Have you heard anything more about Skye's condition?" I asked.

"I called the hospital this morning. They said she's stable, which is good, but she hasn't regained consciousness, which is bad. They did say they weren't discouraged by her progress at this point. She suffered a pretty severe head injury, but they're hoping she'll wake up once the swelling goes down. In the meantime, Mariah and I are adjusting the best we can."

I curled my legs up under my body. This was one of the most beautiful spots on the lake. I knew I would never grow tired of it.

"Where's Levi?" I asked.

"He went back to his place to get some sleep. He tried to help out, but I could see the crying marathon was really getting to him. He's not used to babies."

"Yeah, he really isn't. I'm afraid I'm pretty tied up this weekend with the Hamlet and now the murder investigation, but if you need anything just let me know."

"Murder investigation? Who's dead?"

I spent the next ten minutes getting Ellie up to speed. I hadn't called her last night because I knew she was dealing with her own stuff, and it seemed she hadn't left the boathouse, so she hadn't heard the news from anyone else.

"Wow, the guy was a major pain in the posterior, but I'm sorry to hear he's dead. Does Salinger have any leads?"

"Oh, that's the best part—Salinger isn't here. He's on vacation and has a sub named Deputy Clueless."

"His last name is Clueless?" Ellie looked doubtful.

"No, it's Lesserman, but it should be Clueless. Apparently because I found the body I'm his number-one suspect. He took me down to the station and questioned me until three a.m. As if I would call in a murder I'd committed."

"I suppose calling in a murder you committed would be a good decoy."

I just glared at Ellie.

"Not that I think you did it," Ellie added. "Although Levi did fill me in on your very public outbursts about Duncan. I guess I can sort of see why the guy suspects you. He doesn't know you the way we do. Has Salinger been informed about what's going on?"

"I called him, but he hasn't gotten back to me. I guess I should check in with Lesserman to see if he's heard from him. I really don't want to get involved in this particular murder case, but I don't want to go to jail either, and I have a feeling if I don't come up with some real suspects Lesserman is going to continue to focus on me."

I watched as all four dogs took off down the beach after a flock of seagulls who were well into the sky before they got anywhere near them. The land between the boathouse and Zak's property was all owned by my grandfather and so was deserted because it didn't provide public access. It always made me happy when the animals in my life were having a good time.

"I don't suppose you can think of anyone who might have wanted the man dead?" I asked.

"I can think of a lot of people who didn't get along with him once he started steamrolling everyone, but I doubt anyone from the committee would actually kill him."

"Do you remember him saying where he was from or where he lived and worked now?"

Ellie frowned. "Not that I can recall. But he must have said when he first introduced himself."

"That's the thing—I don't think he did. I'm going to track down Willa later. I'm sure she must have followed up on him at some point."

I turned my attention to the stroller as Mariah began to fuss. Ellie let out a tired sigh.

"Let me try," I offered.

Normally I'm not all that good with babies, but I had a secret weapon with me today. I called over Charlie. Charlie is a therapy dog and has been trained to be gentle with everyone.

I picked up the baby, who immediately began to scream until I sat her down on a blanket Ellie had spread in the shade. Charlie lay down next to the baby, who immediately stopped crying. She smiled when Charlie put his head near her leg. She grabbed a handful of hair and pulled, but Charlie lay perfectly still. After a minute Charlie lifted his head and the baby laughed.

I kept an eye on the pair as Ellie and I continued our conversation. The baby seemed to be happy and content as long as Charlie was next to her. Luckily, the other three dogs weren't a bit interested in the baby and continued to play on the beach.

"I hate to think what's going to happen when you leave," Ellie commented. "More importantly, when Charlie leaves."

"I'm going to be in town all afternoon. I can leave him here if you want. Bella and Digger will be fine on their own. In fact, if you want, I can take Shep with me. It might be easier with just Charlie. I'm afraid Shep will want to play with Charlie when the other dogs leave."

"I think I might take you up on your offer. I think Mariah and I will be fine once she gets used to me, but in the meantime Charlie is a wonderful buffer. Do you think he'll mind staying?"

"No. Charlie is a nurturer. He's in his element when he has someone or something to take care of. I can stop by to pick him up at the end of the day, after you get Mariah to bed for the night. I can bring Shep back then as well, if you want. Or if it's easier, he can stay at my place. Whatever works for you. I take it Levi has Karloff at his place with him."

"Yeah. I'll have Levi leave him at his place if he comes by, which, to be honest, I sort of doubt he will." Ellie had a faraway look on her face.

"Don't read more into this than you should," I warned her. I knew Ellie had a tendency to analyze things a lot more than she really should.

"Don't read more into the fact that the man I'm in love with doesn't like babies?" Ellie asked. "It's always been this huge thing between us. I know I most likely won't be able to have children myself without having surgery, but I still want them. Someday. With the right man."

"Levi just needs time to get used to the idea. And he will. Eventually. Remember, I was the other friend who didn't know what to do with babies and kids under fourteen. Look at me now. I'm a surrogate mom to three kids and I just handled your crying baby without having hysterics. I'm getting to be a pro at this parenting stuff."

"So what do you think changed?" Ellie asked. "What made my never-wants-kids friend evolve into the woman who's sitting with me here today?"

I thought about it. "Nothing about me changed, really. Alex opened my mind to having children, and Zak made me want to be the woman he deserved. Once I got over my kid phobia and tried it, I realized I was actually pretty good at it. Not Zak-good. No one is Zak-good at parenting. The guy's a natural. I try, but I still have my clumsy moments, like when I terrorized that poor little girl at story time. But I'm trying, and I think Alex, Scooter, and even Pi know it. They seem to have patience with my fumbling around at this new role I've taken on."

"The thing is, I don't know if Levi is ever going to be willing to try. He's still pretty adamant about not wanting kids."

"And yet he works with kids every day. Granted they're older kids, but he's good with them and his guys love him. And he's really good with Alex and Scooter. Maybe you just need to get him involved in something with younger kids. I know there's been interest among some of the soccer parents in a football league in Ashton Falls."

Ellie thought about it. "I could see him teaching football to younger kids. It would help him out as well, because it would help to build the skill level of younger kids before they get to high school."

"Mention it to him. And once he masters the younger kids you can ease him toward babies. To be honest, I'm still pretty terrified of the whole baby thing myself, with the exception of Harper, who I adore. Having said that, I very much want to have Zak's babies. Someday. When we're both ready."

I took Bella, Digger, and Shep back to the house, then headed back into town. It was time to talk to Lesserman and come up with a real suspect list. The last thing I wanted was Duncan's death hanging over my head. I was a busy mom with a million things going on each and every week. It would be impossible to try to squeeze in any jail time.

"I'm surprised to see you here today," Lesserman said when I walked in through the front door of the sheriff's office. "Did you come to confess?"

"No, I didn't. Have you spoken to Salinger?"

"I haven't. The man is on vacation. I'll be investigating this case."

I wanted to ask him what he was doing sitting in his office if he was supposed to be investigating, but I refrained from rocking the boat any more than it was already shaking.

"I'm sure Salinger would want to know what's going on. This is his town. He cares about what happens here."

I couldn't believe I was saying that. It wasn't all that long ago that I'd believed Salinger was as useless as Lesserman.

"Salinger is on a cruise. He can't be reached by cell phone for another three days. I'm afraid, Ms. Zimmerman, that you're stuck with me."

Terrific.

"I know you like to nose around and help Salinger, but I don't need nor do I desire your help. Do you understand?"

"Yes, I understand." That didn't mean I agreed.

"Then I'm sure you'll want to be on your way so I can do my job."

"Yes." I smiled politely. "I guess I will be on my way."

I left the office with my fake grin frozen in place. I really didn't have time to break in another clueless law enforcement officer. I had much too much on my plate as it was. There was no way around it; I was just going to have to solve this case on my own.

Chapter 4

I decided the first thing I needed to do was find out who Duncan Wright really was. Someone must know where the guy lived and worked before he appeared in Ashton Falls. It wouldn't really tell me who'd killed him, but it might provide a starting point from which to investigate.

Speaking to Willa seemed to make the most sense. As the official leader of the events committee, she kept track of all the specifics. I knew she was helping out at the Hamlet today; I just needed to figure out where. I tried calling her cell, but she didn't answer, so I headed to Main Street, where the majority of the activities were taking place.

"Have you seen Willa?" I asked Trenton Field, a local psychologist and a new member of the events committee. Trenton was currently helping out in the snack bar.

"Not since this morning. I think she mentioned something about being short-staffed for the haunted maze, so she might have headed over there. I heard about Duncan. You okay?"

"Yeah, I'm fine. I hate to admit it, but I've actually gotten used to finding dead bodies."

"Yeah, but you found this one in a cemetery at night. Sounds like the stuff nightmares are made of."

"Are you trying to give them to me?" I asked.

"Of course not."

"Then don't give me any ideas."

"Want a hot dog or a candy bar?"

Did I? I wasn't really hungry, but I hadn't eaten all day.

"Maybe a hot pretzel," I decided, "By the way, do you happen to know anything about Duncan? Where he lived or worked before he came here?"

Trenton handed me the soft pretzel. "I'm not sure he ever said."

"That's what I thought. I can't remember why we didn't ask."

"Seems like he didn't give us a chance to," Trenton reminded me. "He started off by briefly introducing himself and then he launched right into the first of his ideas. We got wrapped up in conversation about the ideas and never thought to go back to ask questions about who he was or where he was from."

"Yeah, that's how I remember it too. I'm hoping Willa tracked down some additional information after that first meeting. I'm going to head over to the maze, but if you see her, can you tell her I'm looking for her?"

"Absolutely."

It was a beautiful day and I was enjoying my walk through the crowds. I found myself wishing I didn't have a murder to investigate and could simply throw caution to the winds and join my friends and neighbors in the festivities. One of the things I loved most about living in Ashton Falls was that the town made a point of celebrating every holiday and every milestone. It seemed there was always an event in the works that provided a venue for neighbors to spend time together.

The line for the maze was wrapped halfway around the field where it had been set up, but I saw Willa standing at the entrance selling tickets. The maze was really best enjoyed at night, but a lot of families with young children chose to come during the day, when the activity was a lot less terrifying.

"Oh, good, have you come to help?" Willa asked.

I wanted to tell her I hadn't, but she looked swamped.

"Sure, I can help for a while. But I really came by to ask you about Duncan Wright."

Willa pursed her lips. I could tell Duncan wasn't one of her favorite topics.

"Maybe we should step aside. I'll see if Doreen can cover the front gate for a few minutes."

I watched as Willa grabbed Doreen from the apple bob and led her toward the maze.

"What did you want to ask?" Willa said as soon as we stepped away from the crowd.

"Do you happen to know where Duncan lived and worked before he moved to Ashton Falls?" I asked.

"As far as I can tell he didn't. Work, that is. Of course he lived somewhere. After he became so involved in our group I asked him that very question. He gave me a vague answer, so I looked into it some more. I couldn't find any records to indicate he'd had a job. I did, however, find out that since he came here he'd been living in a trailer out at the old Devil's Den mining site."

"Really? Why?"

"I don't know. I just recently found out that bit of information and I never did have a chance to ask him about it. I guess now I never will."

Why would anyone want to camp out at the old mine? It was totally barren, and Ashton Falls had several nice campgrounds closer to town. Unless he was hiding out from someone or something, but if that was the case, why would he join the events committee? The whole thing made no sense.

"Did you happen to find out where he lived before he came here?" I asked.

"I don't have a clue. I guess we should have found out more about him before we welcomed him into our fold," Willa admitted.

"Okay, then why do you think he wanted to help out with the committee in the first place?" I asked.

Willa narrowed her eyes as she concentrated on my question. "If I had to guess," she eventually said, "I'd say he wanted access to things he wouldn't have otherwise."

"What do you mean access? Access to what?"

"He came to me after he'd pretty much taken over and asked to see blueprints of the town before it was redeveloped. He said he wanted to incorporate the history of the place into his story times, which, as you remember, were his idea in the first place. I thought the request odd, but the blueprints aren't exactly off limits to the public, so I took him back to the storage room. While I was there with him I got a phone call. I was only gone for a few minutes, and when I came back Duncan was still standing over the plans we'd been looking at when I left, but I got the sense that something had been disturbed. It was just a feeling, and I let it go. I've thought about that a lot since the day it happened, and I think Duncan used my familiarity with him to permit a situation in which I felt comfortable leaving him in the room while I answered the phone. If he were a complete stranger I never would have left him, even for a minute."

"Who was on the phone?" I asked.

"No one. Whoever was on the phone hung up as soon as I answered. The call was blocked, so I was unable to use caller ID to check it."

"Did you find the incident odd at the time?"

"Not really. I get hang-ups all the time, so I didn't give it a second thought."

"And you were only out of the room for a couple of minutes?"

"If that."

I had to wonder what it was Duncan had wanted access to that he couldn't have just asked about, if that was indeed his motivation for everything he'd done.

Willa and I chatted a bit longer. She didn't have a clue what he was after or even if he was after anything at all. And she reminded me again that the feeling that he wanted access to the room for some reason other than the one he'd stated was only a hunch.

The lines began to decrease as dinnertime approached so I decided to go talk to Hazel, the town's librarian and the second most likely person on the committee to ask questions about the holes in Duncan's past. The library was usually closed on Saturdays, but she was holding a special book sale as a fund-raiser, so I knew I'd find her there.

I wondered how Zak and the kids were doing. I'd fully intended to hook up with them at some point, but so far I hadn't had the chance. Maybe I'd text Zak so we could arrange to meet for dinner. I'd been doing a ton of running around, so I was burning bushels of calories, but I hadn't had the chance to eat anything since breakfast except the pretzel Trenton had given me.

Hazel had set up her book sale on the front lawn of the library. By this point it looked like most of the books as well as most of the customers were gone, which meant the two of us could chat without interruption. After I greeted the woman who I suspected could one day be my new grandmother because she had been seriously dating my grandfather for quite some time, I asked her the same questions I had just asked Willa. She verified that she didn't know much about Duncan other than what we'd learned as a result of his involvement on the committee, but she did share that he'd requested access to restricted documents from her as well.

"What documents?" I asked.

"He wanted to look at the old photo albums, letters, and mining records from Devil's Den. Due to the delicate nature of the items, I keep them locked in the back room. I do occasionally let people I know look at them, but I never allow strangers access to the back room. Many irreplaceable items have been entrusted to my care."

"Did Duncan say why he wanted to get a look at the documents?" I asked.

"He said he was researching the history of the area for story time. At the time I admired the fact that he would go to so much trouble for a children's story time, but I've been thinking about it since he was murdered, and it does seem odd that he would suggest the story time in the first place and then go to the trouble to do so much research but never sign up to give a single story time himself."

I frowned. "What? He wasn't signed up to do any of them?"

"No. Initially, I assumed he was, but I checked the schedule on Friday morning before the events began and he wasn't assigned to anything. Not a single story time or shift at the maze or the haunted house or anything. It seemed as if he blew into town and completely took over but planned to bail once Haunted Hamlet got underway."

I took a deep breath. It seemed like the entire ruse had to do with Duncan's desire to get a look at old records. Willa was right; his motive for becoming involved with us had nothing to do with the Haunted Hamlet but everything to do with getting to know us so that we as a community would allow him access to documents he would otherwise never have gotten near.

"We need to figure out what he was doing out there at the old mining camp and what documents he was really after. He went to a lot of work to pull off whatever it was he had planned. It must have been something big."

"It seems it might have been something worth dying for."

After I left the library I headed over to Donovan's, the general store my dad owns. I doubted he knew anything more about Duncan than Hazel and Willa, but the store was close by and I figured it couldn't hurt to ask.

Donovan's is a cozy small-town store where the locals not only come to shop but to catch up with old friends and perhaps grab a game of chess or checkers as well. As there was on every day when the weather cooperated, there were a number of friendly matches going on at the tables my dad provided for just that purpose in front of the store.

"Didn't expect to see you today." Dad kissed me on the cheek.

"I'm doing a little investigating while Zak and the kids are playing games and eating junk food. I'm finding it harder than I thought to track down information on the latest murder victim."

Dad and I chatted for a few minutes about how little we really knew about the man. In retrospect, it was odd that no one had thought to ask him more questions than we did. One thing was certain: the next time someone new wanted to join the events committee I was going to slow things down and ask the questions that needed asking.

"Now that Duncan has passed we're going to need to replace him on the Hometown Christmas committee," Dad reminded me.

"I thought you were going to chair it."

"I was, but your mom wants us to go to visit her family in Switzerland over the holidays this year."

I frowned. "You aren't going to be here?"

"I thought she'd talked to you about it. She told me she would. Her family has a big get-together at their place in the Alps and it's been a couple of years since your mom has been there. She wants to show Harper off to all the relatives who haven't met her yet."

What about showing me off to the relatives who haven't ever met me?

"We'll be back to spend Christmas Eve with you, but we'll be gone for four weeks, beginning the week before Thanksgiving. I didn't think I should chair the committee if I was going to be out of the country during the critical planning weeks."

"You aren't going to be here for Thanksgiving?"

"I'm afraid not."

"What about the store?"

"Grandpa is going to cover, along with a couple of temporary workers I plan to hire. I'm conducting interviews next week. In fact, if they work out I'm thinking of keeping them on full-time. I think it's time for me to cut back on my hours a bit. Your mom would like to travel more, and I'd like to be around more often while Harper is growing up."

I had to admit I was disappointed my parents would be away for Thanksgiving. Dad and I had never spent a holiday apart, but my mom had a family we didn't really know and I could see how she might want to spend time with them. I guess Harper was going to enjoy the benefits that came with being a Montgomery even if it was too late for me. Still, I had Zak and the kids. We'd be fine.

"I'm really sorry about this." My dad squeezed my hand.

"That's okay. I guess I understand. Mom is proud of Harper. I can see why she would want to show her off."

"Mom is proud of you too. She wanted to invite you, but she knew the kids had school and you would be busy with the Academy."

"Yeah, she's right. There's no way Zak and I could be away for four weeks. Maybe another time."

I knew I shouldn't let the situation bother me. I had my own family now and didn't need to spend every holiday with Dad. But for some reason all I wanted to do was cry.

"Long day." Zak pulled me into his arms when we finally got home and got everyone settled. By the time we'd finished at the Haunted Hamlet we were all too tired for an elaborate dinner, so we'd picked up takeout and brought it home. Then I remembered I needed to go get Charlie and return Shep to Ellie, so Zak got the younger two kids to bed while I did that. Poor Ellie looked exhausted, but she'd managed to get Mariah to sleep, and it looked like the tired baby might sleep through the night. She still hadn't heard from Levi, and Skye still hadn't regained consciousness. I could tell Ellie was at the end of her proverbial rope, so I offered to stay with her overnight so I could help with the baby, but she swore she'd be fine.

Charlie was happy to be going home; he wasn't used to being away from me for long periods of time, but I offered to bring him back the next day if Ellie thought it would help. She thought she and Mariah might come to the park with Zak, the kids, and me for the concert. I offered to pick her up if she decided to attend. It would be good for both her and Mariah to get some fresh air.

"I feel like I could sleep for a week," I agreed with Zak's assessment. "At least we don't have to be anywhere tomorrow until midday. I think the kids are exhausted as well."

"They both went out like a light," Zak confirmed.

"Did you know my parents are going to Switzerland for four weeks?" I asked.

"Your mom mentioned it. I would have said something, but she asked me to let her tell you. I'm kind of surprised it took this long."

"She didn't tell me. My dad did."

"I take it that upset you?"

I shrugged. I was trying to be more secure and mature now that I was married with children, but Jealous Zoe was sometimes still lurking just around the corner.

"She asked if we wanted to go," Zak explained. "I told her that I couldn't really get away, but if you wanted to go with your parents…"

I put my head on Zak's shoulder. "I don't really want to go. And I can't imagine being away from you and the kids. I guess I just felt like the *other* daughter when Dad first mentioned it. Harper is going to grow up knowing her Montgomery grandparents, aunts, uncles, and cousins. Other than my grandparents, who terrified me when I was a child, I never had the opportunity to meet the rest of the family."

"I'll take you to Switzerland anytime you want," Zak assured me.

"I know. I'm just being Zoe. Did Pi make it back home?"

"Not yet."

"Should we be worried?"

"Why should we be worried? He called to check in, and as tired as we are, it's only eleven. We agreed that he'd check in and that he'd be home by midnight on the weekends unless other arrangements had been made and he's stuck to that," Zak said.

"Yeah. It's just that Alex mentioned to me that Brooklyn told her Pi had been hanging out with a kid she classified as bad news."

"Brooklyn has a tendency to act possessively toward Pi," Zak reminded me. "They seem to enjoy hanging out, but if you ask me, she's a lot more serious about the relationship than he is. I think we should listen to what she has to say but look for other motives as well."

"What do you mean?" I asked.

"Pi's new friend is taking him away from Brooklyn. It's possible she's simply jealous and trying to convince us to discourage the relationship. Pi's a good kid. I think we should trust him to make his own decisions until such a time when he does something to show us we shouldn't."

"You're right. You've really nailed this parenting thing."

Zak smiled. "So how am I doing with the husband thing?"

I rolled over so I was looking Zak in the eye. "I'm not sure I'm totally satisfied, now that I think about it. Maybe you should do something about that."

Zak pulled me on top of him. "Maybe I will."

Interactive Reader Portal: This book contains a story within a story. Phyllis's thoughts are included as a separate story at the end of this book. If you want to read the story chronologically, read chapter 4 of *Zimmerman Academy* now. Once you finish reading it, return to the top of Chapter 5 of the main story, and you can continue on from there. If you prefer to read *Zimmerman Academy* as a separate story, or if you prefer to skip the chapters narrated by Phyllis, continue on to Chapter 5 now.

Chapter 5

Monday, October 26

"My grandparents want me to come to the farm for Thanksgiving," Scooter announced as I drove him to school.

"I see." Why was it that I was suddenly feeling deserted? "I'm sure it will be nice to see them. It's been a couple of months. Will your dad be there?"

Scooter shrugged.

"Well, Zak can arrange for you to go visit your family either way. Did they say how long they wanted you to come for?"

"Grandma said I should come when school lets out on the Friday before Thanksgiving week, and then I can come back the Sunday after Thanksgiving. She said Alex could come with me."

"Did you ask Alex if she wanted to go?" I wondered.

"She said she would if it was okay with you."

I wanted to say no, it absolutely wasn't okay with me, but I wasn't *really* Scooter's mother, and it was perfectly reasonable that his actual grandparents would want to spend time with him. And while Alex wasn't related to them, Scooter would have a lot better time if Alex went along.

"If Alex wants to go then that's fine with me. I'll talk to Zak today about scheduling Coop to take you and bring you back."

Coop was a private pilot Zak often hired.

"It looks like it'll just be Zak and Pi and me for Thanksgiving."

"Pi is going to that band thing."

"What band thing?" I asked.

"I'm not sure. Just some band thing. He said he talked to Zak about it and it was okay with him."

I found it odd that Zak hadn't mentioned anything, but perhaps he was still looking into it. I pulled up in front of the school.

"Don't forget to ask your teacher about the spelling words you're supposed to be studying."

"I will," Scooter promised as he opened the car door.

"And please be sure to find out when your class is going to the Children's Museum. Your teacher said she would send home a note, but so far I haven't seen it."

"Okay."

Scooter slammed the door.

"Love you," I said to the boy who was halfway to the school building.

I turned to Charlie. "Should we go see Jeremy?"

He barked.

"Yeah, I think so too."

Charlie and I headed to the Zoo. I hadn't spent nearly as much time as I'd like with the animals I'd committed to care for as of late. Jeremy Fisher and Tiffany Middleton, who worked for me full-time, were great. I knew the animals were fine as long as they were in their care; it was I who suffered when I stayed away too long. I love my family more than I can say and being a wife to Zak and a surrogate mom to Pi, Alex, and Scooter was very rewarding, but I needed to have my time with my four-legged friends.

"Fantastic concert yesterday," I said to Jeremy as we walked in the door. Charlie trotted over to greet Jeremy, who was standing at the front counter, playing with two of the kittens we were getting ready to adopt to a new family.

"Thanks. I thought it went well," Jeremy answered as he bent over to pet my small sidekick. "Pi has turned out to be a huge asset. I know you have plans for him that go beyond the Rock and Roll Hall of Fame, but he has real talent."

"Yeah, he really is good. Zak is grooming him to work for him when he graduates college, but young adults don't always stick to the career path the authority figures in their lives choose for them. Pi does seem to enjoy working with Zak, so I guess we'll see if he can stay serious and out of trouble."

"Any particular reason why you think he might not?" Jeremy asked.

I shared with him what Brooklyn had told Alex.

"I don't know the kid Pi has been hanging out with, but he hasn't said anything to me that would indicate that he was doing anything that might get him into trouble. I'll keep an eye on the situation." Jeremy laughed. "I can't believe I'm saying that. It wasn't that long ago when *I* was the one getting into trouble."

I picked up one of the kittens, who had decided to attack my shoelaces. What was it with kittens and shoelaces?

"You're a father now," I pointed out. "Being a parent changes your perspective."

"Yeah, I guess so."

"Has Pi said anything to you about a band thing over Thanksgiving?"

"Yeah. Some of the guys in my band are going and they invited him. He seemed excited about it, and the guys will make sure he stays out of trouble. I mentioned it to Zak and he said he thought it would be fine."

"Yeah, it sounds like fun. Pi seems to really get along well with the guys in spite of the age difference."

"Pi's easy to get along with and he has a good head on his shoulders. He's good with kids too. Morgan loves him."

Jeremy had a point. Pi did seem to have his head on straight these days. I'm not sure why I was being such a worrywart.

"Morgan certainly was having fun at the concert yesterday," I commented. "Mom and Dad joined us, and when you guys started in with that new song you've been working on Morgan, Harper, and Alex were all dancing around in a circle."

"I'm sorry I missed that."

"I took a video. I'll forward it to you. I'm trying to be better about catching adorable family moments on film. By the way, are you and Morgan coming to the Zak and Zoe Halloween spooktacular this year?"

"We are," Jeremy confirmed. "We're meeting up with your parents to take Morgan and Harper trick-or-treating first. I think Phyllis and the girls might join us. We'll be by when we're done."

"Great. I'm superexcited about it this year. I was going to ask Ellie to do the food again, but she has her hands full with Mariah. Maybe I'll ask Kelly if she can help out."

Kelly Arlington was Ellie's assistant at the Beach Hut, the lakeside restaurant Ellie owned.

"Ellie seemed to be doing better with Mariah yesterday," Jeremy commented.

"Yeah. I think the baby is getting used to her, which makes the whole thing easier. I noticed Levi didn't show, like I hoped. I feel like I should have a talk with that guy."

"Best friend or not, I wouldn't," Jeremy counseled. "Trust me, Ellie and Levi need to work this baby thing out between them. I know you love them both and want them to be together, but this is a major issue. I think it's a good thing for them to each decide where they really stand before they make a commitment and then regret it."

I sighed. "You're right. I can't believe you're better at this relationship stuff than I am."

"Not better, just more objective. I've been meaning to ask you if you've made a decision about the cat family at your house. It might be time to begin looking for homes for them."

Alex and I had found a cat in the process of having kittens seven weeks earlier. We'd helped the mom to deliver four healthy babies who had been living in one of the extra rooms at the house ever since. I knew Alex was attached to them, but we already had three dogs and two cats. The last thing we needed were five more cats.

"I'll talk to Alex. I know she'd love to keep them all, but that isn't practical. I'd be open to allowing her to keep either the mom or one of the kittens. Once she decides what she wants to do, I'll bring the others down so we can begin looking for homes for them. They really are cute. I bet we'll have no trouble placing them."

Jeremy picked up one of the kittens and placed it in the travel crate we supplied to our adoptive families. "When these two little darlings leave we'll be completely out of kittens. Which is a good thing. We only have two adult felines to place, so I'm sure the kittens you have at the house won't be here long."

"Did the guy who wanted to adopt that lab mix check out okay?" I wondered.

"He checked out great. He's coming by to get her this afternoon. I think I found a home for the sheltie as well. A good one, with lots of room for him to run."

"Wonderful. I guess I'll head back and check on the wild animals. Call me if you need me."

The Zoo was built to have two distinct sections. Three, if you counted the small animals, which were caged in the center of the building, to the right of the area for domestic animals. Each dog had their own kennel, with both an indoor and outdoor component. There's also a play area where the social dogs could play.

The cat area was designed as sort of a lounge. Felines who got along with others were allowed to roam freely in the large area that was equipped with climbing posts and pillows to lounge on. Kittens and their mothers were kept in the nursery.

In the center of the building were cages for squirrels, birds, and other small animals. To the far left was the area where we kept the larger wild animals such as bears, mountain lions, and coyotes. We currently had five bear cubs and two injured coyotes in residence. We released our injured and orphaned animals as soon as they were able to survive on their own.

"Hey Zoe; Charlie," Tiffany greeted us. "I'm glad you're here. That cub from the Riverton fire has been acting lethargic the past couple of days. I first noticed it on Friday, and when I came in to relieve Gunnar this morning he confirmed that he'd been off his feed. I called Scott and he said he'd stop by, but I thought you'd want to know."

Scott Walden was our local veterinarian.

"I do. Thanks."

I walked over to the cage in which the cub was housed and looked in on him. Poor thing. He'd been through a lot. He seemed to be doing better, so I hoped that whatever was wrong was no more than a temporary setback.

"How's the murder investigation going?" Tiffany asked.

"It's not. I really want to track down Duncan's killer, but I was busy with family stuff the entire day yesterday."

"That's good. Your family should be your priority. What does Salinger think?"

"Salinger is out of town. There's a sub up from Bryton Lake who seems to think I did it."

"You? Why?"

I shared some details of my very public tirades in the day or two before the murder.

"Yikes. That really does make you sound guilty."

"Tell me about it. I was furious with the guy. A lot of other people were too, but I was more vocal about it. I've pretty much determined that the best way to divert suspicion from myself is to find the real killer, but I'm not sure where to start."

Tiffany opened the bear cage and tossed in some fresh fruit. "Most times the best place to start is with what you know."

I explained what I'd learned from Willa and Hazel concerning Duncan's interest in documents he'd only been able to access due to his familiarity with the women. I also shared that he was camping out at the old mine and that he didn't appear to have any intention of actually helping with the Haunted Hamlet in spite of the fact that he all but took it away from me.

"Have you been out to the mine?" Tiffany asked.

"No, not yet."

"Seems to me to be as good a place as any to start."

Tiffany was right. It *was* a good place to start. I explained what I was doing to

Jeremy and then Charlie and I headed out of town on the old highway. After the mine was closed the road that led to it had fallen into disrepair, leading to a paved surface that was riddled with potholes. I found myself wishing I'd left the cute little car Zak had bought me at home in favor of my huge four-wheel-drive truck.

In spite of the treacherous road the drive was absolutely gorgeous. The fall leaves were bright and plentiful and the contrast of the yellow with the evergreen trees that grew in the area was breathtaking. When we arrived at the clearing where the old mine offices were located I spotted a trailer, which I assumed belonged to Duncan, off in the distance. I parked the car and exited the vehicle. Charlie and I looked around the area, which appeared to be deserted, before we started off down a recently trod-upon path that would lead us to the trailer.

The entrance to the old mine was a good five hundred feet higher in elevation than the town. The breeze blew through the valley, creating a wind tunnel affect near the mine. I wrapped my arms around my waist as I struggled to stay warm in air that was much cooler than that which I'd recently left.

The first thing I noticed when I approached the trailer was the yellow tape across the door. Apparently, Lesserman had beat me to the punch. I stood on tiptoe and looked in the window. The entire interior of the trailer had been trashed. Everything had been pulled out of the cupboards and drawers and deposited on the floor. Had Lesserman done this, or had he found it that way when he arrived? One thing was certain: someone was looking for something.

I took a few steps away from the trailer and looked around. If I had something to hide I certainly wouldn't keep it in the trailer. The security of the interior was nonexistent, and unless I planned to be on the premises twenty-four/seven, I think I'd find a more secure location for my treasure. I'd want to keep it close enough so I'd be able to keep an eye on it but also far enough away so as not to make it conspicuous.

I considered the mine shaft halfway up the nearby mountain. Too obvious. The old buildings at the entrance to the mines might make for a better hiding spot. I hadn't really stopped to check to see if anyone had accessed them lately. I slowly turned in a circle, considering my surroundings.

It was totally quiet up here on the mountain except for the sound of the wind whistling through the valley. I knew the larger forest animals preferred the isolation of the higher elevations and wouldn't be at all surprised to find I was being watched. Charlie stood next to me, his ears tipped forward, always on alert yet unmoving.

"What do you think?" I asked my furry friend. "If you wanted to hide something where would you put it?"

Charlie took off at a run, traveling into the thick brush as the foot of the steep trail that led to the mine shaft. I ran after him, hoping all the while that there wasn't a predator lurking nearby. Charlie was a smart and brave, but he was a little dog and therefore not able to defend himself from the coyotes and cougars I knew lived in the crevices of the rocks above.

When I caught up with Charlie he was frantically digging at a piece of plywood that had been buried under a layer of dirt. The plywood turned out to be a door, under which I found a small but deep hole. At the bottom of the hole was a metal box. I reached in to grab it but found it much too heavy to lift. I'd need leverage. I looked around for something to use as an aide. I had a rope in the car that I tied to the box and then found tree branches with which to create a sort of pulley system. It took some work, but I managed to leverage the box to the surface. Of course the box was locked, but with a little effort I managed to get it into the car.

"Let's go home," I said to Charlie, who was growling at something in the distance. "I'm almost sure I saw a pair of eyes watching from the crevice just above that ledge. I'm not sure I want to find out who they belong to."

Charlie barked once and jumped into the passenger seat.

Chapter 6

By the time Charlie and I finished up at the mine it was time to pick Scooter up from school. Both Alex and Pi attended Zimmerman Academy in the afternoons, so they came home with Zak at the end of the day. I found I really enjoyed the two hours Scooter and I had for just the two of us each day.

"I got an A on my math test," Scooter announced as he climbed into the passenger side of the car.

"Awesome." I put my hand up for a high-five.

"That's the third A I got in the past two weeks."

"I know. I'm so proud of how well you're doing. You're working hard and it shows."

"Do you think if I keep getting As I can go to Zimmerman Academy with Alex and Pi?"

I hesitated. We'd discussed the matter with all the kids and I'd thought Scooter understood why he wasn't participating in the Academy, but apparently I was wrong on that front.

"I didn't think you wanted to go to the Academy. In fact, I specifically remember you saying you wanted to be in Tucker's class."

"I do want to be in Tucker's class, but he got an A on his test too. We both want to go to the Academy."

"Why don't we see how things go this year and then we can take another look at it in a year or two?" I suggested. "I know Miss Maxwell is very excited to have you in her class, and she depends on me to be class mom. I don't think we want to let her down."

"Can't I do both? Pi and Alex do both."

Scooter had a point. Both Pi and Alex went to public school for half a day and then to the Academy in the afternoon.

"Yes, but Alex is in middle school and Pi is in high school. I don't think it would work to do the half-day thing in elementary school. Maybe when you get into middle school we can work something out."

Scooter frowned, but he let it drop.

"Did Miss Maxwell give you the spelling list we needed?"

"Yup."

"And did you find out about the field trip?"

"She said she was going to e-mail you the information. I think it's in a week. Maybe two."

"And did she give you a list of what we need to bring for the class party on Friday?" I asked.

"It's in my backpack. She said punch and cupcakes would be fine, but I want to do goodie bags too."

"Goodie bags?"

"Little bags like we had for my birthday, only with something scary on the front and things like candy and rubber spiders inside. Everyone does cupcakes, but I want us to have the best party."

"I think we can do goodie bags," I agreed. "We can stop off at the costume shop if you want. I noticed they had a whole area with stuff for Halloween parties."

Scooter smiled. "Okay."

I made a left and headed back into town.

"What's in the box?" Scooter asked, as he noticed the box on the backseat for the first time.

"I'm not sure. Charlie and I dug it up at the old mine. We're going to take it home and open it. Want to help?"

"Okay. After we get the spiders and stuff."

We bought a whole bag of candy, spiders, plastic teeth, and other trinkets, then headed home. I gave Scooter a snack and went in search of tools to open the box. It had a sturdy lock on it, but I knew Zak had something in the shed that would cut through the lock. Zak actually had a lot of tools, which he used mainly for his holiday decorating obsession. When Scooter and I had pulled up we'd noticed the work he'd started on the yard that morning. Zak not only wanted the inside of the house to have a Halloween feel but the outside as well. It had actually been Zak's decorations and my destruction of said decorations that had led to my identifying a killer the previous Halloween. Maybe Mr. and Mrs. Frankenstein would work their magic again.

Just looking at the Mr. and Mrs. Frankenstein figures gave me the chills. Sometimes you think you know someone and then you realize you never really did at all. I didn't want to think that Duncan's killer was known to me, but experience had shown that most victims of violent crime were attacked by someone they knew well.

"Did you find it?" Scooter asked when I returned to the house.

"I did." I held up the bolt cutters.

It took a little elbow grease, but I managed to get the box open.

"Wow, look at all that stuff," Scooter exclaimed.

The first item at the top was a large manila envelope, which was filled with photos of maps, blueprints, and documents. If I had to guess, taking photos of the archives in the county offices was what Duncan had been doing when Willa left the room to answer the phone. Fortunate coincidence or did Duncan have a partner?

Below the first envelope was another one with old photos. I wondered if these came from the albums Hazel kept in the library or if Duncan had another source. First thing tomorrow I'd head to the library and find out.

Below the photos was a one-way ticket to Rio. It was in Duncan's name and the flight was scheduled to depart the following week.

Below the ticket was a letter, written in a language other than English, that looked like it was at least a century old. I'd have to ask Alex about it when she got home. She was familiar with a wide range of languages thanks to the fact that she was both brilliant and had traveled extensively.

"Do you think the letter is really a treasure map?" Scooter asked. "Because that would be awesome."

"I suppose it could be. I guess we'll see if Alex can read it when she gets home."

"What's for dinner?" he asked, apparently growing bored with the contents of the box.

"I'm not sure. I know Zak was going to do something with those leftover chicken breasts. We can try to figure out what he made and see if we can make something to go with it."

I put the cheesy casserole I found in the refrigerator in the oven and then started on a salad while Scooter buttered the loaves of sourdough bread. While Zak did most of the cooking in our house, on school nights he tended to prepare something ahead of time that just needed to be heated, so Scooter and I had taken to getting things started while we waited for the others to get home.

"Can Tucker come to the Halloween party on Saturday?" Scooter asked.

"I already sent an invitation to his mom."

"Can he spend the night?"

"I guess that would be fine, as long as you promise to go to sleep and not play around all night like you did the last time Tucker stayed over."

"We want to watch scary movies on my TV. Tucker says it's a tradition in his house to watch scary movies on Halloween."

"Okay, but not too scary. I don't want the two of you waking up with nightmares."

"We won't."

I looked out the kitchen window. "Zak just pulled up. Why don't you go wash up and then set the table?"

"It's Latin," Alex said later that evening after we'd finished eating and I shared the contents of the box with the others. "Basically, it's the last will and testament of a man named Alvin, written to a man named Isaac. The document is dated July 12, 1915, and it appears that this Alvin wanted Isaac to travel to a specific location to retrieve 'that which he left behind.' The instructions are vague. Probably intentionally so," Alex added.

"Vague how?" I asked.

"For example, the man who wrote the letter states that Isaac should look for the first clue in the spot where Aunt Matilda had afternoon tea."

I frowned. "So the clues were personal and could only be followed by the recipient of the letter."

"Probably." Alex nodded.

"So no treasure?" Scooter was obviously disappointed.

"I guess not, buddy." Zak patted him on the back.

"Do you think this Isaac could be Isaac Wainwright from the legend?" I asked.

Alex looked at me. "The dates line up. The legend states that Isaac died on October 23, 1915, while looking for a stone. Maybe this Alvin was a relative and Isaac came to Devil's Den to find what he'd been left, only to be murdered for his trouble."

"It seems like a long shot," Zak contributed.

"Yeah, but even long shots are possibilities," I reminded him. "And most legends have an element of truth behind them. It might not have happened exactly like the story, but I'm betting something significant happened to cause the legend to come into being in the first place."

"Okay, say it is true. Say Isaac was a real person who really did come to Devil's Den to find a treasure. How did Duncan get hold of Isaac's letter?" Zak asked.

"Duncan's last name is Wright," I realized. "What if Wright is a shortened version of Wainwright? I suppose it's possible Isaac didn't actually bring the original copy of the letter with him when he came. Or if he did, maybe he realized he was in danger and mailed it to another relative. Perhaps Duncan's grandfather?"

"Okay, then let's assume Duncan came to Ashton Falls to pick up where Isaac left off. Why all the subterfuge?" Zak asked. "He had the letter, which would have given him a plausible reason to simply ask Willa, Hazel, and whoever else he may have talked to for access to the old records. Why would he come to the area, set up camp near the old mine, and get involved with the events committee? It makes no sense."

"Yeah, and who killed him?" Scooter added.

Later that evening, after the kids were settled in their rooms, we went into the sitting area of our own room with a glass of wine. I really enjoyed this time we spent together most evenings. Life seemed to have become so hectic that we rarely had time to relax. Charlie was asleep at my feet, Bella was lying by the fire, and Marlow and Spade were curled up in the bed. It was times like these, when it was just us, that I found the link to who we were before the kids and the Academy and our wonderful but hectic new life.

"It looks like we're going to be totally deserted for Thanksgiving." I brought up the subject that had been on my mind since I'd talked to Scooter that morning.

"I take it you spoke to the kids."

"I talked to Scooter. He told me that he's going to his grandparents and Alex is going with him. He also told me that Pi is going to a music event. Jeremy confirmed that he'd been invited. How come you knew all this and I didn't?"

Zak set his glass down on the coffee table, then turned so he was facing me. He took my hand in his before he began to speak.

"The thing with Pi wasn't a for-sure thing until today," Zak began. "I spoke to a couple of the guys in the band and we worked out the details. I think the weekend will be good for Pi. It will give him something to think about besides the fact that his mom isn't with him this year."

"Yeah. I guess I can see that," I acknowledged. Pi's mother had passed away during the past year.

"And as far as Scooter and Alex, I planned to talk to you about it this evening. Originally, I was going to talk to you about it yesterday, but you seemed so upset that your parents weren't going to be here that I decided to let you get used to that idea first before I brought up the situation with the kids."

I leaned back into the sofa. I didn't say anything, but I was sure Zak could see the unhappiness on my face.

"I know you're disappointed that everyone is going to be gone. I am too. But it did occur to me that we might be able to use the fact that we'll be alone to our advantage. As much as I love our new big noisy life, we have very little time for just the two of us."

I frowned. "Advantage how?"

Zak handed me a brochure for a gorgeous resort that promised world-class skiing, spa facilities, luxury cabins with river-rock fireplaces, and full kitchens.

I looked at him. "You want to go on vacation?"

"The place is in the Colorado Rockies. It's a world-class resort with first-class skiing, dining, and accommodations. We never really did have much of a honeymoon, so I thought we could drop Scooter and Alex at Scooter's grandparents and then spend a week with no interruptions. No work, no Academy, no kids, and no murder."

I looked down at the brochure. The resort had sleigh rides, ice skating, and snowmobiling in addition to skiing. The cabins were situated right on a lake that was frozen over in the winter but still beautiful.

"Just the two of us?" I confirmed.

"Just the two of us. And Charlie."

"It does sound nice."

Zak pulled me into his arms and kissed my neck.

"It would be fun to ski on runs that are new to us," I commented. "Are you sure they allow dogs?"

Zak paused and looked at me. "They do in the cabins. I already checked."

"The spa does sound nice," I added as Zak returned his lips to my neck.

"Hmm."

"And the food looks delicious."

Zak moved his mouth lower.

"And the cabin seems cozy."

Zak ran his hand up my leg.

"And the bed looks…"

Zak captured my lips and that was the end of the conversation.

Chapter 7

Tuesday, October 27

I wasn't sure why we were even having an events committee meeting this morning because we were between events, but Willa liked us to meet every week, so most times we did just that. I was a few minutes early because I'd needed to drop Scooter at school on my way, so I ordered a muffin to go with the coffee Rosie provided for the weekly event.

Rosie was famous for her muffins, featuring a selection that changed with the seasons. Today I was able to choose between cranberry nut, cinnamon apple, and pumpkin spice. I chose the pumpkin spice. It was, after all, just four days before Halloween.

"I heard about Duncan," Jennifer, the cashier, said as she rang up my purchase. "I have to say I'm not surprised in the least."

"Why do you say that?" I asked as I added an apple strudel to my order.

"There was something unnatural about the guy. He gave me the creeps. I could almost have predicted that he'd die in a cemetery."

"Unnatural?" I wondered.

Jennifer leaned in so she could speak without being overheard and lowered her voice to the point that I could barely make out what she was saying. "The guy had a weird aura. It seemed cloudy and unsettled. Like he wasn't really who he was, if that makes any sense."

It didn't.

"And his friend was just as unsettled," Jennifer continued. "I'd almost be willing to bet neither man was entirely human."

"What friend?" I asked, deciding not to get into a discussion as to why the men might not be human. Jennifer had a very open mind and was more willing to believe in aliens, zombies, and ghosts than the average citizen of Ashton Falls.

Jennifer shrugged. "I don't know his name; he was just a guy Duncan met for lunch a few times. Actually, I guess it was just twice. Once about three weeks ago, right after Duncan started coming in here, and the other time was last week. I think it might have been Wednesday. Or possibly Thursday. The guy was an odd egg."

"Can you describe him?" I asked.

"Tall, thin, freakishly pale. If you ask me, the guy looked like he lived in a cave, or maybe a mine. It looked as if his skin had never even seen the sun. And his eyes were very odd. I would totally believe he was a vampire, but they met during the day, and you know vampires are creatures of the night."

"You said his eyes were odd. Odd how?"

"They were dark. Almost black, and they had this hollow look. It almost seemed like they didn't have irises."

The man Jennifer was describing could be the one I saw in the cemetery. I hadn't seen his face, but he was tall and thin. Of course I suppose a lot of men were tall and thin.

"Did you ever overhear their conversations?" I asked. "Even small parts of one? Maybe while you were refilling beverages?"

Jennifer appeared to be considering my question as she stared into space. "I know the tall man wanted something from Duncan. I'm not sure what. I overheard him say there would be consequences if he didn't deliver *it* on time. I also know

Duncan and the man fought when they were in here last week. I couldn't hear what was being said because they had already gone out to the parking lot, but I could tell by their body language that they were arguing."

"And you have no idea who this man was?"

"No. Like I said, I don't think he's from the area."

"Did the men pay with cash or credit card?" I waved to Willa and Hazel, who had just walked in and were heading toward the back room where the meetings were held.

"Cash. Duncan paid and he always paid in cash."

"Okay, thanks. Let me know if you think of anything else."

I took my coffee and snacks into the back room. I wanted to have a chance to share what I'd found in the lockbox with the women before everyone else arrived. I had a feeling neither of them was going to be happy that Duncan had repaid their generosity and willingness to let him access the records he was after by stealing from them.

I sat down at the conference table and shared what I had found in the box. While both were irritated with Duncan, Hazel was also clearly intrigued.

"What sort of clues were in the letter?"

"Alex didn't read them all, but the ones she did seemed random," I answered. "My guess is that the letter was written to a family member who would understand the significance of the clues. It's actually a smart strategy because it provides the information the relatives would need to find whatever was left for them while affording a level of protection should the letter fall into the wrong hands."

"Can you remember an example of a clue?" Hazel asked.

"There was something about finding a clue where Aunt Matilda had tea. A person would obviously have to know this Aunt Matilda to even make a guess."

"Not necessarily," Hazel responded. "I've studied the photos in the albums quite extensively and I seem to remember there was a teahouse in Devil's Den."

I frowned. "A teahouse? Really? I sort of pictured Devil's Den as being more a saloon town than a tea town."

"Devil's Den had plenty of saloons," Hazel assured me. "But after some of the miners married and moved their families to the area other types of enterprises sprang up. I'll need to look at the photos again to be sure, but I think the teahouse was in the approximate location where Trish's Treasures sits now."

"This is beginning to sound like the Dollinger treasure all over again," I pointed out. "You don't think Duncan was after the same thing that got Pack Rat killed, do you?"

"I'm not sure," Hazel admitted. "It does seem as if there are similarities between the two series of events."

"The letter is pretty much the only clue I have at this point. I'll take another look at it to see if the clues do line up with places that are findable in modern-day Ashton Falls."

"I'd be happy to help if you'd like," Hazel offered.

"Maybe Alex and I will come by the library later. I can pick her up from the Academy early. I'll bring the old photos I found so you can see if they were taken from your albums."

"I intend to inspect the books as soon as this meeting is over," Hazel assured me.

"I'd be interested in knowing which documents Duncan photographed from my office as well," Willa informed me.

"I'll bring the photos by," I promised.

Willa looked at her watch. "It looks like we might be the only ones to show today."

"I guess people are busy this week," I offered. "And we don't have any events until the community dinner at the end of November."

"I suppose it wasn't imperative that we meet today," Willa admitted. "I planned to go over the profit and loss statement for Haunted Hamlet, which is depressing to say the least. What I don't understand is why Duncan bothered to trash the haunted house. He already had the documents he needed from Hazel and me. Why did he even show up at the event at all? It makes no sense."

Willa was right; it didn't make sense. You would think if the man was treasure hunting he'd keep a low profile rather than calling attention to himself by showing up at the Haunted Hamlet and tossing a monkey wrench in the whole thing. Something definitely wasn't adding up.

After the meeting I decided to stop by Ellie's Beach Hut to ask Kelly about the food for the spooktacular. I supposed I could do it myself, but I wasn't much of a cook and I really didn't have any extra time to devote to the party. When I arrived I found Ellie behind the counter and Mariah asleep in the portable crib my mom had lent her.

"I didn't think you'd be in this week," I said.

"I still have a restaurant to run."

"I just figured you'd let Kelly handle things while Mariah was with you," I explained.

"I fully intended to, but Kelly had another run-in with her boyfriend and had to have stitches put in her eyebrow."

I grimaced. "Ouch. I thought he was doing better controlling his aggressive tendencies."

Ellie sighed. "He was. He was going to counseling, and Kelly said he was a lot less volatile, but he hit her when she came home the other night. She told me she has no idea what brought on the attack and she swears she's done with him for good."

"Hasn't she said that before?"

"Yeah, I know. I don't understand the psychology that allows her to forgive him time and time again, but it's been her pattern and I'm not sure this time will be any different. I encouraged her to press charges, but she refused. I really like Kelly and I feel bad about her situation, but I may have to replace her if she continues to take the guy back. I need someone I can depend on to be here when she's scheduled to work."

I sat down at the counter. The restaurant was deserted, but it was a little early for the lunch crowd, and Ellie wasn't open for breakfast during the off season.

"Maybe she really will leave him this time," I offered.

"Maybe." Ellie looked doubtful. "But even if she does, she's going to be out for the rest of the week. I'll just have to see how things go."

"Have you heard anything more about Skye's condition?"

"Her body is healing and she seems to be doing better than expected in some ways, but she still hasn't woken up. Her roommate seemed a lot more concerned that she might not wake up than she was the last time I spoke to her. I called to try to talk to the doctor myself, but he was in surgery, so I left a message. I feel so bad for Mariah. She really misses her mama."

I glanced across the room to the crib. The baby looked like she was sleeping peacefully, but I knew she was having a hard time with the situation.

"Is she sleeping better?" I asked.

"Yeah, she seems to be. It seems like we're starting to settle into a routine. Did you stop by for something to eat? I just realized you didn't know I was here, so you didn't stop by to talk to me, and you don't usually come in just to chat with Kelly."

"Actually, I did come by to talk to Kelly. I wanted to ask her if she would be willing to do the food for the party on Saturday."

"I thought I was doing the food."

"You were, but I figured that now that you have Mariah to take care of you wouldn't have the time or energy."

Ellie pulled a sheet of paper out of the drawer under the cash register. "I've already made a list of the food to serve and the ingredients I'll need. And I spoke to Zak, who'll be doing the grocery shopping, and Alex and your mom have agreed to help put everything together. Hazel called to offer her services as well, and Phyllis said I should just give her holler if I needed someone to watch Mariah while I cooked. I think we have it handled."

I smiled. "Great. I can help if you need me."

"No offense, but we don't."

"My cooking isn't that bad," I covered.

"I didn't say it was. I just figured you had a full plate with the whole murder investigation. Did you ever talk to Salinger?"

"No. I left a message on his cell, so I guess he'll call me when he gets into an area with service. I did find a map buried in a box."

I spent the next fifteen minutes catching Ellie up on the murder case, the list of suspects, which was depressingly sparse, and the possibility of buried treasure.

I looked at the crib, where Mariah was starting to stir.

"Let me take Mariah for a few hours," I offered. "Ninety percent of your customers come in over a three-hour period, and I'm sure Mariah and I will be fine for three hours."

Ellie looked hesitant.

"I used to babysit Harper when she was this age," I reminded her.

"Yeah, with Zak's help."

"I'm perfectly capable of handling one baby on my own for a few hours. I have some errands to run and I planned to pick up Charlie anyway. Mariah loves Charlie. We'll be fine."

Ellie glanced at the clock and then at the crib. "Are you sure you don't mind?"

"Positive. I'm picking Alex up early from school and meeting with Hazel later today, so I'll bring Mariah back at around three."

"That really would help. Thank you."

"That's what best friends are for."

Ellie fed and changed Mariah before we left. After her nap Mariah was cheerful and alert, and I felt confident we could make it for a few hours on our own. I picked up Charlie as planned and then headed into town to do a few errands. Twenty minutes into the venture Mariah and I were both in tears. Not wanting to bother Ellie, I did the only thing I could: I headed to the Zoo and Jeremy.

"Why all the tears?" Jeremy asked as Charlie, Mariah, and I came into the shelter through the front door.

"She won't stop crying. I don't know what to do."

Jeremy reached for the baby, who stopped crying the minute I passed her to him.

"How'd you do that?" I asked in amazement.

"I didn't do anything. You, my friend, are a bundle of nerves and uncertainty. Babies pick up on that. You need to relax and she will too," Jeremy counseled.

"I thought I *was* relaxed."

Jeremy took my clenched hand in his.

I looked down at the tension in my entire arm. "I only got tense after she started to fuss."

Jeremy swept the baby's hair out of her eyes. "Maybe you should see if your mom has time to babysit," Jeremy suggested.

"My mom. Of course. She'd be happy to help, and that would provide a solution for Ellie until she figures out what's going to happen in the long run. Why didn't I think of that?"

"I guess you've been preoccupied with everything that's been going on."

"I'll call my mom right now."

I'd headed into my office to do just that when my phone rang. It was Salinger. "Thank God you got my message," I said.

"What have you gotten yourself into this time?"

"None of this is my fault," I defended myself before explaining exactly what I'd gotten myself into.

I could picture Salinger frowning as I explained what a huge mess his incompetent sub was making of things. I hoped Salinger would see the wisdom of abandoning his vacation and taking the next flight home.

"Sounds like Lesserman is doing things by the book," Salinger replied.

"By the book isn't going to cut it," I argued. "There's something really strange going on here. I mean, the fact that the killer was dressed like some sort of creepy monk makes this case unique in and of itself."

"You're certain the man you saw was the killer?" Salinger asked.

"No, I guess I'm not sure," I admitted. "But why else would he be in a graveyard late at night?"

"You said you saw the man, screamed, and then tripped over the body. What did the man who was dressed like a monk do?"

"He didn't do anything. He disappeared. One minute he was there and the next he was gone."

"Had you been drinking?"

"Of course I hadn't been drinking," I spat. "I saw what I saw. The man was real."

"Did he have a weapon?" Salinger asked.

"Not that I saw."

"Did he attempt to assault you in any way?"

"No, I told you, I ran when I saw him, and when I looked back toward where he'd been standing he was gone."

"So he could very well have just been someone passing through."

"He was dressed like a monk," I pointed out.

"It's Halloween," Salinger reminded me. "Maybe he was one of the cast members from the haunted house. Maybe he was walking home from a party."

I took a deep breath. I hated to admit it, but Salinger had a point. The man hadn't done anything but scare me. He could have been anyone. Of course he did take off, even though I'd tripped over a body. Why wouldn't he stay to help unless he was the killer?

Chapter 8

Luckily, my mom was free the entire week and agreed to keep Mariah while Ellie was at work, which made for one less thing for both of us to worry about. Mom had gotten a late start on the job of mothering, but she seemed to have taken to it like a duck on water once Harper was born.

"Thanks, Mom. I really appreciate this." I hugged my mom when I stopped by to hand Mariah off. "Ellie really appreciates this too."

"It's no problem. I'm more than happy to help in any way I can. Poor Ellie really has a lot to worry about, it seems. First her cousin's auto accident and then her assistant gets sick."

I'd decided not to burden my mom with the real reason Kelly was going to miss work that week. I knew Kelly liked to keep her abusive relationship a secret, and I also knew my mom would feel compelled to intervene if she knew what was going on. My mom wasn't the sort to sit idly by if she felt there was an injustice to be righted, whether she personally knew the individuals involved or not. The more I thought about it, the more convinced I was that I probably *should* fill Salinger in on the situation when he returned.

I let out a sigh of relief when I saw that Mariah was smiling and happy to be in Mom's arms. Until it occurred to me that she seemed to be smiling and happy when she was in anyone's arms other than mine. Why did babies hate me?

"I take it you're working on the murder case?" Mom asked.

"Trying to," I answered as I put the diaper bag on her kitchen counter. "I'm afraid I'm not really getting anywhere. I'm picking Alex up from the Academy and we're going to head over to the library to work on some ideas with Hazel. Maybe something will come of it."

"It seems like you have a new sleuthing crew for this one."

I laughed. "I guess I do. Zak would help if I asked, of course, but he's busy with the school and his new client. Ellie is already on overload and Levi has been AWOL since the baby arrived."

"AWOL?" Mom asked.

"Not literally. He's still in Ashton Falls, it's just that I haven't seen him since the day Ellie brought Mariah home. I don't think he's doing well with the whole baby thing. I'm a little worried about how this will affect Ellie and Levi's relationship, but that's a discussion for another day."

"Well, I'm sure Hazel and Alex will make excellent sleuthing partners."

"They will, especially because the letter we're investigating is written in Latin. Ellie will come by to pick up Mariah when she gets off and then she'll bring her by in the morning on her way to work." I kissed my mom on the cheek. "Thanks again for doing this."

"Baby." Eighteen-month-old Harper had toddled into the room while Mom and I were talking.

My mom knelt down so she was on the same level with my little sister. "We have to be gentle with the baby."

Harper reached out a hand and Mariah grinned. I wished I could stay and watch the little ones play. Although they were a year apart in age, I could see the two baby girls were going to get along just fine.

"Dad told me about Switzerland," I commented. "It seems Zak knew as well. I'm kind of surprised you didn't tell me about your plans."

"I was going to," Mom assured me. "It's just that I knew this would be your first holiday without your dad and I felt bad about that. I talked to Zak because I hoped he would tell me that of course you could all come along with us, but as I suspected that wasn't the case. I really would like to go see my family, but I kept waffling when it came to making a firm commitment. I don't want you to feel deserted."

"I don't feel deserted." Actually, that was exactly how I felt, but I wasn't going to say as much.

"My mother wanted us to stay through the New Year, but I told her that I absolutely had to be back in time to spend Christmas with both my girls."

I smiled. "I'll be fine. Really. I have Zak now, so I'm sure I won't miss Dad as much as I otherwise would have. And I'm glad you'll be home for Christmas. Go see your family and have a good time."

Mom hugged me. "You're quite the exceptional person."

"Right back at you."

After I left Mom's I headed back into town to pick up Scooter from school. My plan was to drop him off at the Academy with Zak and then pick up Alex, who was predictably excited to help me with my treasure hunt. If the clues that had initially seemed personal in nature actually did correspond to actual landmarks, maybe we could follow where they led and possibly find out what Duncan had been after.

As soon as Alex and I arrived at the library Hazel spread both a current map of Ashton Falls and a historical one out on the table. The trick would be to convert the clues, which we now theorized would pertain to landmarks, into their modern-day equivalents. To aide in our research, Hazel had piled old photo albums on a nearby table. We hoped that between the maps, the photographs, and the letter, we could figure out what Duncan was up to. And maybe if we could figure out what he was after, and who he might have run in to along the way, we could figure out who'd killed him.

As Hazel had suggested, the first clue referred to the old teahouse. Now that we knew the clue was relevant, Alex and Hazel worked to translate the letter a bit more thoroughly. Part of the problem they were having was that the letter seemed to be written using terms expressed in both Latin and a very old English dialect. Luckily, both Alex and Hazel were well versed in languages and seemed to be working it out.

"It seems like the clue refers to the position of the front door of the teahouse in relation to the building," Alex commented.

Hazel managed to find a photo of the building as it had existed in 1915.

"I think you're right," Hazel agreed. "If I'm reading this correctly, the writer of the letter wanted the recipient to stand in the threshold and look into the distance."

Hazel compared the photo to the historical map.

"Here." She pointed to a spot on the map. "If a person stood in the doorway here and looked toward the horizon and the distant summit, they would have been looking at an area that would fall pretty much along this line."

"That's the old logging road," I supplied.

"I believe you're right," Hazel agreed.

I can't tell you how proud I felt to actually be helping the two brainiacs I was working alongside. Up to this point all I'd really been able to contribute was to hold down the corners of the old map.

"The second clue refers to Jacob's fork," Alex provided.

"There's a peak here called Jacob's Peak," Hazel said.

"Jacob's fork must refer to the intersection where you can head west toward the peak, south to town or north toward the old mine," I mused.

Alex, Hazel, and I continued to translate the letter and then apply it to the map using old photos.

"'Wilbur's mistake'?" Alex translated. "At least I think it's mistake. The clue seems to point toward something pertaining to a mistake, or maybe a problem. If we translate it as problem it could even suggest a different sort of problem, like a math problem. The sentence is sort of mangled. It almost seems as if the person who wrote the letter didn't quite know how to express what he was trying to say."

"Let me see that." Hazel reached for the letter. She read it over several times, jotting down some possible translations. She wrote down the words: mistake, problem, error, dilemma, dispute, issue, obstacle, trouble.

The possible translations for the word could have a similar meaning, but they could also have very different meanings as well. For example, if the intended word was mistake and we read it as problem we would still find the intended message. But if we read the word as problem and the intended word was obstacle we could end up looking in the wrong direction. I wondered how we would hone in on the intended meaning if the specific word used had both Alex and Hazel stumped.

"The clue must refer to a landmark," Hazel stated. "The others did."

"Folly," I said. "I saw something in one of these photo albums about Wilbur's Folly."

I opened the book in front of me and began thumbing through the pages. I couldn't remember which book it had been in, but there had been a photo of a man standing in front of a pile of dirt that had been labeled Wilbur's Folly.

"Here." I pointed to the picture. It didn't show a lot of background, so it was hard to determine where it had been taken. I wasn't sure if it could help us even if my theory was correct.

"I remember something about Wilbur's Folly," Hazel said. "I need to go into the back to get a book."

"This is fun," Alex said while Hazel was gone. "Maybe I'll get a job with the CIA when I get older."

"I thought you wanted to be a veterinarian."

"I did. I do. I'm not sure. When we helped to deliver the kittens last month it seemed like the most perfect job, but now I'm not sure."

"You're ten. You have time to figure it out."

I looked up as Hazel walked back into the room, reading as she went. I hoped she wouldn't trip. I probably would if I tried to walk and read at the same time.

"It says here that a man named Wilbur Fortnight came to the area with the fortune he'd inherited from his grandfather. He didn't really need the money mining would bring, but he had the fever and was determined to find his share of the gold in the area. The other miners knew he had money, so they came up with a plan to make him think he'd found a rich vein when all he'd really found was dirt. They planted gold in his mine and then sold him the equipment he would need to excavate at ten times the normal rate. In the end he died a broke and broken man."

"That's sad," Alex commented.

"I'm thinking the clue must refer to the location of the mine," I said.

Hazel looked at the map and then back at the book. She frowned as she considered the information. "It's hard to say exactly, but I think the mine was about here." She pointed to a spot on the map.

"I know where that is. If nothing else, we can drive out there to see if there's evidence of an abandoned mine."

"I don't mind closing a half hour early," Hazel said. "Not a single person has come in while we've been working."

"Okay," I decided. "Let's take a drive to see what we find."

The drive out of town was pleasant, whether we found the mine or not. The temperature had grown chilly as the sun began its descent, but with the thrill of the chase none of us even noticed. At the appropriate place I turned from the highway onto an overgrown dirt road that was little more than a trail at this point. The road wound up the mountain until we ended up on a flat surface. An abandoned mine shaft was evident farther up the mountain. We'd have to continue on foot, which none of us was willing to do.

"Well, there was definitely a mine here at one point. I'm not sure how we can tell if this is the one referred to in the letter."

"It's really cold up here and it will be dark soon," Hazel pointed out. "Maybe we should continue this quest another day."

"There's only one clue left," Alex told us. "It refers to a home of the dead."

"It's the old Devil's Den cemetery," I realized. The cemetery was clearly visible from where we stood. "Alvin wanted Isaac to go to the old Devil's Den cemetery."

"I think you're right," Hazel agreed.

"But why? Does the letter say why?" I asked.

Alex looked down at the paper in her hand. "It looks like the letter continued onto a second page, but there was only one in the envelope you found."

"So the question is, did Duncan ever have the second page?" I asked.

Alex and Hazel both stood quietly as we contemplated the possibilities. If he'd had the second page, could he have hidden it away from the first so the treasure couldn't be found if someone were to find just one page or the other?

"What if he didn't have the second page," I suggested after a minute. "What if the letter he had led him to the cemetery but not to the treasure? Perhaps that's why he trashed the haunted house. He knew he needed to come back after dark when he could search for the treasure without drawing attention to himself, so he trashed the house so we would be forced to send everyone home."

"Why wouldn't he just wait until Monday, when the haunted house was over?" Alex asked.

Good question.

"He must have been in a hurry for some reason," Hazel theorized.

I remembered that Jennifer had said the tall man Duncan had had lunch with wanted something from him and had threatened him with consequences if he didn't deliver on time. Could the consequences he'd referred to be a cleaver to the head?

"Penny for your thoughts," Zak said later that evening. We were curled up on the sofa in the sitting area of our bedroom. Zak had gone out of his way to create a romantic setting with a fire in the fireplace, soft music, pumpkin-scented candles, and a bottle of wine that probably cost more than I made in a year.

"Even you can't afford my thoughts tonight," I teased.

Zak tucked a lock of my hair behind my ear. "Long day?"

"The longest. Don't get me wrong; I actually enjoyed my treasure hunt with Alex and Hazel, but I'm not sure discovering why Duncan might have trashed the haunted house brings us any closer to finding his killer."

Zak put his arm around me and pulled me next to his body. I always felt safe and warm when I was with Zak. I don't know if it was the fact that he was so tall or that he was so intelligent, but I knew in my heart that he would always find a way to save me when I got myself into trouble. I suppose in a way having this confidence in my man made me more fearless than I really ought to be.

"Why don't you tell me what you do know?" Zak suggested.

"I know there was a man in the cemetery with a black-hooded robe the night I found the body. I suspect he's the killer, but Salinger did make some good points when I talked to him today."

"You talked to Salinger?"

"Yeah. Sorry; I thought I'd told you. He was in port, so he was able to return my rather frantic call. I hoped he'd help, but he was totally useless."

"Useless in what way?" Zak asked as he ran a finger up and down my arm.

"He seems to think Lesserman is conducting an adequate investigation, which he isn't. I just think Salinger didn't want to have his vacation interrupted."

"Can you blame him?"

"No. I guess not." I leaned my head against Zak's shoulder. I did find that I was beginning to relax.

"Okay, so you have the guy in the cemetery as a suspect. Who else?"

"Jennifer from Rosie's said she saw a tall, thin man arguing with Duncan. It could be the same guy I saw in the cemetery. The cloaked man was tall, but it was hard to make out any other features. I also suspect Duncan's death might be related to the letter and whatever it is he was after in the cemetery."

Zak kissed the top of my head, which was resting under his chin. "Do you think he found it? Whatever it was he was looking for?"

"I have no idea. I guess I should see if Lesserman will tell me what was found on or near the body. I sort of doubt he will. I really wish Salinger was here."

Zak laughed. "Did you ever think you'd be saying that?"

"No." I smiled. "I guess not. At least I didn't ever imagine I'd be saying that until recently. The guy had me fired from my job two years ago."

"Yeah. But that worked out okay."

"Yeah, it really did."

I turned and looked up into Zak's eyes. They really were the most expressive eyes. They promised things I knew we'd share and hinted at things I could only imagine. I wondered if our children would inherit his kind heart and patient spirit. I hoped so. The world really could benefit from a little more Zak in the mix.

Chapter 9

Wednesday, October 28

Zak decided to commit a couple of hours to my investigation the next morning, so I took the kids to school while he logged onto his computer and began the process of tracking down the elusive Duncan Wright. Zak was a wiz on the computer, so I knew that if there was something there, he'd find it.

When I returned home from dropping everyone off I joined Zak in his office.

"So what do we know?" I asked.

Zak sat back in his chair. "Quite a bit, actually. Duncan Wright is the only son of Reginald Wright, a native of Pennsylvania. Reginald is the son of a man named Byron Wright, who came to this country from England when he had a falling out with his father, Lucifer. Byron changed him name to Byron Wright from Byron Wainwright when he came to the United States."

"So Duncan *was* related to Isaac Wainwright," I concluded.

"It looks like he was. In 1915 when Isaac died he left behind a son who was five years old at the time. His name was Lucifer. It appears Isaac was Duncan's great-great-grandfather. There's no way to know for certain how Duncan ended up with the letter you found, but it seems likely it was handed down from one generation to the next."

"So Duncan must have had reason to believe Isaac never found whatever it was Alvin sent him here to find and decided to come to Ashton Falls to have a look for himself," I concluded.

"It seems as reasonable a theory as any," Zak agreed.

"Is this Alvin related to the Wainwrights?" I wondered.

Zak turned back to his computer and typed in a series of commands. "According to the letter you found, the correspondence was the last will and testament of a man named Alvin Everlay. I don't know this for certain, but I think he might have been the son of the Duke of Everlay. I was able to verify that the duke had a son named Alvin who would have been around fifty in 1915."

I frowned. "So we suspect Alvin was the son of a duke who came to Devil's Den at some point prior to 1915. He must have known he was dying because he sent

Isaac the letter. Isaac would have been what age in 1915?"

"Thirty."

"Okay, so he would have been twenty years younger than Alvin. I wonder how they knew each other."

"I haven't been able to find a link between Alvin and Isaac so far," Zak said. "I'll keep looking. If Alvin is the son of the duke, as I suspect, I guess we can assume both Alvin and Isaac were from England. I suppose they could have been friends or neighbors."

He swiveled around in his chair so he was looking at me. "While establishing a link between Isaac and Duncan is interesting I'm not sure how it helps us identify his killer."

"The only thing I can come up with is that Duncan was after whatever it was Alvin left for Isaac and someone found out about it and decided they wanted it for themselves. If whatever Alvin left behind is the motive for Duncan's murder I'm not sure how we're ever going to figure out who else might have known what Duncan was up to."

"The guy was a tool, but I'm sure he had friends. If not in Ashton Fall then wherever it is he came from just before moving here."

"I thought you mentioned Pennsylvania."

"Duncan's father was from Pennsylvania. I haven't found a record of him living there, or anywhere else for that matter, as an adult. I'll keep looking."

I stood up. "Thanks. I appreciate it. I think I'm going to head over to the Zoo for a couple of hours."

"By the way," Zak stopped me, "Phyllis and the girls are having a Halloween dinner party tonight. Phyllis said it's casual and she'd like us and the kids to come."

"Sounds like fun. What time?"

"Six."

"I'll be ready."

I decided to stop by Rosie's on my way to the Zoo. Maybe she or one of the waitstaff could give me more information about the man Jennifer had seen Duncan arguing with. At this point my stranger in the graveyard and the man in the diner were the only leads I had. The one thing that had stuck with me was the fact that Jennifer had indicated that the man Duncan was speaking to wanted something and he wanted it quickly. Urgency was the only explanation I'd come up with as to why Duncan might have trashed the haunted house on Friday.

"Yeah, I know who you're referring to," one of Rosie's newer waitresses told me. "I'm pretty sure I heard Duncan Wright refer to him as Gus. I didn't catch a last name. Based on what I managed to hear while I was clearing the adjoining table, it seemed Duncan owed Gus some money. Quite a lot by the sound of things."

"Any idea where I can find Gus?" I asked.

"I don't know for sure, but I remember one of the men mentioning the Bayside Marina."

I knew the Bayside Marina was on the south shore of the lake. It was about a thirty-minute drive from Ashton Falls, but I didn't have to be anywhere until it was time to pick Scooter up, and that was still four hours away.

"Okay, thanks. If you think of anything else give me a call."

I left the café and returned to my car.

"Want to take a ride?" I asked Charlie, who had been waiting for me while I was inside Rosie's.

It had been quite a while since I'd driven around the lake. It was a beautiful drive, with the narrow road hugging the lake, with its beaches and rocky shore. It was a warm and clear autumn day. There was a nip in the air, just enough to remind you that winter was on the way.

The Bayside Marina was one of the larger ones on the lake. Not only did they rent and store boats but they had a boat ramp, a marine store, and a full-service repair center. It turned out Gus worked there as a mechanic. I knew I'd found the right guy when a tall, pale man approached me.

"What can I do for you?" he asked.

"My name is Zoe. I live in Ashton Falls and I'm looking into the death of Duncan Wright."

The man pursed his lips. "You a cop?"

"Not exactly, but I often help Sheriff Salinger with the research for some of the cases the department works on. I understand you had lunch with Duncan recently."

"Yeah. So?"

"I understand that the two of you argued."

The man frowned. "You think I killed him?"

"Not necessarily. Duncan argued with a lot of people. I am, however, interested in the reason for your argument. I have a witness who seems to think Duncan owed you something."

"He did. Money. A lot of it. The lowlife had been stringing me along for months. I realized I was going to have to threaten to get rough if I ever wanted to see my dough again."

"Did you?"

"Did I what?"

"Get rough?"

"No. Thought about it, but the guy said he had a plan to get my money, so I decided to give him some more time. Guess he was getting some sort of inheritance. Suppose I never will see that money now."

"Probably not. Do you know of anyone else Duncan owed money to?"

Gus paused. It appeared as if he was seriously considering my question. "Duncan liked to gamble. I imagine he probably did owe other people money. I know for sure that he owed a big chunk of change to a guy named Ford. Don't know his last name."

"Do you think this Ford could have killed him over the debt?"

He shrugged.

"Do you know anyone else who might have wanted to kill him?"

"Lots of folks. The guy had an annoying way about him. But if what you're really asking is if I know who killed him, the answer is no. You might ask his girl."

"Duncan had a girlfriend?"

"Sweet but misled little thing named Analee."

"Do you know where I can find Analee?"

"Diner down the street. She doesn't always wear a name tag, but you can't miss her. She has the bluest eyes you've ever seen."

"Blue eyes. Got it. Thank you for your time."

Charlie and I decided we might as well have a chat with Analee as long as we were in the area so we headed down the main street toward the intersection, as Gus had instructed. It occurred to me that if Duncan had a girlfriend on the south shore of the lake that was most likely where he lived. I had to wonder why he'd been camping out at the mine. Even if he was trying to find a treasure he could easily have made the trip back and forth each day. It was an easy drive during the summer and fall, when there wasn't any snow to contend with.

When I got to the diner I asked Analee that very question.

"Duncan was hiding out," Analee shared. "He'd somehow managed to talk himself into inclusion in a high-stakes poker game, and when he lost he didn't have the money to cover his marker. He made a lot of really mean men a lot of promises that he was never going to be able to keep."

"Gus said Duncan told him that he had a plan to get the money he owed. Do you happen to know what it consisted of?"

Analee looked around the diner. It was slow, but I could tell she was uncomfortable discussing Duncan if others were within hearing range.

"He had an inheritance coming to him," she whispered. "A big one. He just needed to find something to get the money."

I frowned. "Did he tell you what he needed to find?"

"No, but he assured me that once he found whatever it was, he and I were going to move away and start over somewhere tropical. Just the two of us. Duncan said he loved me, but he hated the snow."

Gus was right; Analee was adorable. I couldn't imagine what she would want with a guy like Duncan.

"During his time in Ashton Falls he became very involved with our events committee. Did he tell you why?" I asked.

Analee hesitated.

"He's dead," I reminded her. "He can't get into trouble for doing whatever it was he did."

"Duncan needed some information. When he first arrived he tried to get it, but he was told it was restricted, so he got the idea to make nice with the ladies from the county and the library."

So Willa had been right about that.

"He also wanted access to the house you all were using for some event. He said the thing he needed to find was most likely there, so he needed a reason to be given a key to the place."

And it appeared I'd been right about the clues in the letter leading to the cemetery.

"Do you think Duncan found what he was looking for?" I asked.

"Not unless he found it after the last time I spoke to him, which was on the Wednesday before someone killed him. I heard the man who killed my Duncan was lurking around in the cemetery. I surely hope you find him. It was supposed to be just the two of us. He promised we'd have a future together and now he's gone."

The poor girl looked like she was actually grieving. I couldn't imagine why someone like Analee would have had anything to do with someone like Duncan, but I suppose love can be blind. Duncan was a first-class tool, but he must have done something kind at some point to win Analee's heart.

"Do you know someone named Ford who Duncan owed money to?"

"Yeah. Ford Olson. He lives over on the east shore. He's a real scary guy. Do you think he killed my Duncan? I bet he did. He's just the sort to kill a man."

"I don't know whether Ford killed Duncan, but I'd like to talk to him. Do you have an address for him?"

"No, but I can draw you a map to his place."

After I left the diner I called Zak to fill him in on what I'd learned. He would be busy at the Academy for the rest of the afternoon, but he promised to give the information some thought. Charlie and I filled the car up with gas and then headed toward the east shore. Ford was a scary-looking man, but he swore he hadn't killed Duncan and he had an alibi of sorts. He also told me Duncan had said he'd found a gold mine and would be paying everyone back sooner rather than later. This seemed to back up what both Gus and Analee had already told me.

After we finished with Ford Charlie and I headed north toward home. By the time we arrived back in Ashton Falls I needed to rush to pick up Scooter.

"Zoe, can I get another costume?" Scooter asked the minute he got into the car.

"I thought you liked the one we got for you."

"I did. But Tucker and Percy are both going to be ninjas. I want to be a ninja too."

I was about to tell Scooter he'd made his choice and he really needed to stick with it, but then I got a look at his face. This was really important to him.

"Okay. We can run by the costume store to see what they have, but we'll need to hurry. We're going over to Phyllis's for dinner."

"Okay. I'll hurry."

The store was predictably packed. It was, after all, only three days before Halloween. Apparently, a lot of people had left shopping for a costume until the last minute. At least I'd been in the store enough times lately to have a feel for which costumes were located in which section. The action-type costumes were on the back wall, so we headed there directly.

Scooter picked out the costume he wanted and we headed to the end of the long line. By the look of things I wasn't going to have a lot of time to get ready for the dinner unless they happened to open another check stand. I was about to ask them to do just that when I remembered there was a cash register in the back, at the layaway counter. I took Scooter's hand and headed back to the rear of the store again. Of course, trying to maneuver there was a bit like swimming upstream, but I put my head down and plowed through.

"Hi, Zoe, how can I help you?" the clerk asked.

"Can you ring this up back here?" I asked. Hopefully she would or I'd lost my place in line for nothing.

"We're really only supposed to do layaways and returns here, but after all the help you gave me when my boxer got lost I'm happy to break the rules. Just let me finish ringing in this return."

I looked at the costume in the clerk's hand and gasped. It was the exact same robe I'd seen the man in the cemetery wearing.

"You sell these robes?"

"Yeah. They're monk costumes. Do you need one for Zak? This is an extratall."

"No, Zak has a costume. Do you happen to know who returned this?"

"Evelyn Straw. Her husband Fred was going to wear it, but his cousin died, so they're going to be out of town this weekend."

I knew Fred Straw. He was a nice guy and I seriously doubted he was the man who'd scared me in the cemetery.

"Do you know who else bought this costume?" I asked.

"It depends. If they have an account with us and they slid their discount card when they bought the costume we'd have a record. If they used a credit card we'd have a record. If they paid cash and didn't have an account with us we wouldn't have one. Why do you ask?"

"I can't go into detail, but it might have to do with the investigation into Duncan Wright's murder. Can I get a list of everyone who bought the robe?"

The clerk hesitated.

"It's important."

"I guess it couldn't hurt. But don't tell my boss I gave it to you. He tends to be prickly about things like that."

The clerk handed me the list as soon as it was printed. There were five names, including Evelyn Straw's. "Do you know how many of these robes were in inventory?" I asked.

The clerk looked it up. "We ordered seven."

"And were they all sold?"

"We have one on hold for Dover Wood and the one that was just returned by Evelyn. The rest are no longer in inventory."

If there were seven robes and I had five names, including Evelyn's, that left Dover and one other. "So there's one that's unaccounted for."

"Like I said, we don't keep track of cash customers unless they slide their card. We don't have a lot of cash sales, but they do occur from time to time."

If Dover hadn't picked up his costume yet it couldn't have been him I saw in the cemetery. I knew everyone on the list the clerk had handed me and couldn't really see any of them being a killer, but someone had been lurking around on the night I'd found Duncan's body. It would be just my luck that lucky number seven was the man in the cemetery, but I would be remiss if I didn't at least have a chat with each and every one of the five people I did have.

Interactive Reader Portal: If you want to read the story chronologically, read chapter 5 of *Zimmerman Academy* now. Once you finish reading it, return to the top of Chapter 10, and you can continue on from there. If you prefer to read

Zimmerman Academy as a separate story, or if you prefer to skip the chapters narrated by Phyllis, continue on to Chapter 10 now.

Chapter 10

Thursday, October 29

"You're up early," I said to Alex the next morning. She was sitting at the kitchen counter staring into space. I could tell she had something important on her mind. Alex was a serious person who tended to have serious thoughts.

"I'm trying to decide what to do about the cats."

I'd spoken to Alex the previous evening about the fact that it was time to find homes for the feline family we'd been housing.

"This is the hard part about fostering animals," I admitted. "In the process of caring for them you come to love them, and when it's time to say good-bye it creates a void."

"It's going to seem so weird when they're gone," Alex said. "I've gotten used to getting up in the morning and going in to check on them first thing. And the kittens are so cute. And fun."

"If you want to keep one of the kittens I'm sure we can accommodate one more animal in the house."

"That's what I've been thinking about. While the kittens are supercute, I think Sasha needs us more." Sasha was the name Alex had given to the mama cat. "So if it's okay with you I think I'll keep her and let Jeremy find homes for the little ones."

I smiled. "I think that sounds like a good plan. We'll need to have Sasha spayed so we don't have any more kittens. I'll make the arrangements when I get to work this morning."

"Okay." Alex sighed.

I put my hand over hers and gave it a squeeze. "Is there something else on your mind?"

"I got an e-mail from my mom."

"And something she said upset you?" I asked.

"She said it wasn't going to work out for her and Dad to come back to the States for the holidays. I knew they wouldn't be here for Thanksgiving, which is why I agreed to go with Scooter to his grandparents' farm, but I really thought they would come for Christmas. At first my mom wanted me to meet them in New York, but after I talked to her she said they would come to Ashton Falls instead, so I could show them where I'm living now. It would have been fun for them to be here with all of us for Christmas."

Alex's parents were archaeologists who traveled the world looking for artifacts.

"I'm sorry. I know it's been a while since you've seen your parents."

Alex looked at me. "The thing is, my mom offered to arrange for me to come to South America for Christmas because they couldn't come here. I don't want to go to South America. I want to stay here in Ashton Falls. Now I don't know what to do. If I tell my mom the truth I might hurt her feelings."

Somehow I doubted that. Alex's parents really didn't go out of their way to spend time with her. Last year she would have been left alone at the boarding school she and Scooter were attending if he hadn't brought her home with him. I felt bad that Alex felt bad about feeling the way she did.

"What if you had a really good reason for needing to stay in Ashton Falls over break?" I asked.

Alex looked at me. "Then I could tell my mom that while I would love to come for a visit, I really couldn't because of this previous obligation."

"Exactly."

"What obligation?" Alex asked.

I furrowed my brow as I considered the situation. In order for Alex to stay, as she wanted to, without running the risk of hurting her mother's feelings, which she was afraid she might, she would need a really compelling reason to stay. One that her parents would understand. Something academic-based would be best. It was obvious they put academic achievement above all else.

"Why don't we talk to Zak and Phyllis about it? I'm sure between the two of them they can come up with an important project that requires your attention."

Alex smiled. "Thanks, Zoe."

"I'd better go nudge Scooter out of bed. He seems to be sleeping in later than usual and I don't want him to be late for school."

"He was up late working on his spelling words. He even asked me to help him study. I get the feeling it's bothering him that he isn't as smart as Pi and me. I tried to explain to him that we all have our own talents and he should be proud of the fact that he's athletic and funny."

"Yeah, he said something to me about not being included in the Academy. When we first talked about it he seemed fine with the fact that you and Pi would be spending your afternoons there while he would be attending public school, but now that classes have started I think he feels left out. It really wouldn't work to have him do the half day thing you and Pi do while he's in elementary school, but I'll talk to Zak about some sort of special project he can be involved in."

"I think that would be a good idea," Alex said. "Of course he's so busy with sports after school I don't know when he'd have time to participate in a project, but I do think he needs to feel that he's part of this big thing you and Zak are doing. Maybe he can help Zak with something."

"Like what?" I asked.

"Like maybe a computer game. Scooter likes to play video games. Maybe if Zak has time they can develop one together."

I smiled. "That's an excellent suggestion. I'll talk to Zak about it."

I decided to drop the kittens off at the Zoo that morning. Now that Alex had made her decision it was best to make a clean break. I knew how hard it could be to say good-bye to animals you'd nurtured for weeks or even months. I still remember the devastation I felt when I'd released into the wild one of the first bear cubs I'd rescued. He came to me weighing less than five pounds. I'd had to bottle-feed him until he was able to be weaned onto solid food, and during those first weeks he'd toddled around my office while I worked. I'd even bought him a stuffed doggie to sleep with. I knew in my mind that I couldn't keep him, but he felt more like a pet than a wild animal. When the time came to release him I began to imagine every possible challenge he might face. As I watched him walk into the woods, my heart shattered. I'd cried the entire drive home.

"Are those the kittens?" Jeremy asked when I walked in through the front door of the Zoo with a travel crate.

"All four of them. Alex decided to keep the mama."

"I'm sure we can find the little darlings wonderful homes. How's Alex doing with the separation?"

"Okay, considering. The first time is always the hardest."

"I spoke with her about it last night at Phyllis's dinner. She seemed to really be struggling with the whole thing."

"Yeah. Alex tends to take almost every decision she makes very seriously. I'm afraid at times she overthinks things, but I suppose that's a side effect of superintelligence. Once she came to a decision, though, she seemed to be okay with going through with it."

"I'm glad."

"How's our lethargic cub?" I wondered.

"Scott came by yesterday to look at him. He wants us to put him on a special diet, so I segregated him from the other cubs for the time being. He seems about the same today, but Scott didn't seem overly concerned."

"Did he look at the retriever when he was here?"

"He did. He said the cast should come off in a week."

We'd had a golden retriever brought in about a month before that had been hit by a car. He'd suffered a broken leg and cuts and bruises but was going to be just fine. We never had been able to track down an owner, so we planned to put him up for adoption once he was cleared by Scott.

"I'll take the kittens back and get them settled," Jeremy said.

"Okay. I have a few calls to make and then some leads to follow up on. Is Tiffany here?"

"Yeah. She's in the back."

I found Tiffany cleaning the dog runs. If there was one thing that could be said for having a job at the Zoo it was that there was always something to do. If there wasn't something to be cleaned, there was someone who needed to be walked or fed.

"Hey, Zoe. How's it going?" Tiffany asked.

"Busy. Can't stay long. I wanted to ask if you would be available to stay at the house for a week or so over Thanksgiving."

Tiffany's face lit up. "Really? You know I'm always more than happy to stay at your five-star home. I'm kind of surprised you're going to be away for the holiday, though."

"Pi is going to a music event with some of the guys from Jeremy's band and Scooter and Alex are going to his grandparents'. Zak thought it might be a good time for us to have some couple time, so he made us a reservation at a resort in Colorado."

"Sounds wonderful, although I think if I lived in your house I'd never want to go anywhere else. Is it okay if I have Scott come stay with me?"

"Absolutely. I've been meaning to ask how things are going between the two of you. Not that it's any of my business, but you know I'm nosy."

Tiffany laughed. "Things are going well. I'd say we're dating seriously, and while we're very much exclusive, neither of us has brought up anything more permanent. I kind of have a feeling Scott is working up to that, so I've decided to be patient and let him set the pace. I'd like for him to meet my parents. I was actually thinking about inviting them to Ashton Falls for a few days over Thanksgiving."

"If you decide to invite them feel free to have them stay at the house. In fact, consider the house yours to use as you'd like. We're taking Charlie with us, but the rest of our menagerie will be there to keep you company if you end up wanting some alone time."

"Thanks. I'll think about it."

The first stop I made after leaving the Zoo was the grocery store to speak to Ernie Young, one of the six people who'd bought a monk's robe from the costume shop. I'd called Evelyn Straw from my office, who'd said the costume she'd bought for Fred had never been opened. I offered my condolences for the loss of Fred's cousin and then called the costume shop to confirm that the robe had been returned unopened. That left me with five possible suspects: the other four I had names for and the one who'd paid cash.

"Hey, Ernie," I greeted him as I walked through the front door. One of the awesome things about Ernie's market was that much of the time Ernie was right there at register one to greet you.

"It looks like I get to enjoy a double dose of Zimmerman this morning."

I must have looked puzzled because Ernie continued, "Zak was in earlier buying supplies for your Halloween party."

"Oh. Good. I'm glad he remembered because it totally slipped my mind. I hope you'll be able to stop by."

"Plan to. I have a costume and everything."

"Awesome. What are you coming as?"

"A psycho killer."

I frowned.

"I bought a monk's robe and a Jason Voorhees mask at the costume shop."

"Oh. It sounds like a scary costume. Have you tried it out? I thought I saw someone dressed like that on Friday."

"Wasn't me. I was in Bryton Lake with the family for the weekend. Might have been Jim you saw. He mentioned that he might try his costume out at the Haunted Hamlet. We ended up buying the same robe, but he has an ape mask instead of a Jason one."

"Yeah, it was probably him."

"So what can I help you with today?" Ernie asked.

"Help me with?"

"I'm assuming you came in to buy something."

"Oh. Yeah. I did." I picked up a candy bar and set it on the counter. "Midmorning munchies," I explained.

After I paid for the candy bar I really didn't want but still somehow ate, I headed toward Jim's Taco Hut. Of the men on the list, Jim seemed the most likely to become violent, although none of them really struck me as being the killer. Still, if I had to choose between Jim, Ethan Carlton, and Dr. Ryder Westlake, Jim would be my man.

"Here for a taco?" Jim asked as I walked through the front door.

"Uh, yeah, I could do a taco."

I was going to gain ten pounds by the time I finished this investigation.

"Did you go to the Haunted Hamlet over the weekend?" I asked.

"I went on Sunday. I had to work until closing on Friday after one of my guys didn't show up and I had tickets for a concert in the city on Saturday. Shame about the haunted house. I was really looking forward to it. I even planned to wear my *Planet of the Apes* costume."

"Yeah," I agreed as I accepted the taco and began pouring hot sauce over it. "It really was a drag that the haunted house was closed before it even got started. Not only were there a lot of disappointed people but we lost a lot of revenue. I'm sorry you had to work late on Friday. It was really rocking downtown."

"By the time I got off at eleven most of the fun was over. Oh, well, maybe next year. Can I get you anything else?"

"No. This will do it. Thanks."

If Jim had worked until eleven on the night I saw the hooded man in the graveyard it couldn't have been him. The problem was that all I was left with was Ryder Westlake, Ethan Carlton, and the man or woman who'd paid cash. I seriously doubted either Ryder or Ethan would hurt a flea, although I didn't know for sure that the masked man had killed Duncan. It was possible someone else was the murderer and the masked man just happened to be wandering around the graveyard. Still, either Ryder or Ethan would have stopped to help me when I fell. Additionally, either man would have tried to help Duncan had they noticed the body.

While I didn't believe either man could be guilty, it seemed prudent somehow to speak to them before officially crossing them off the list. I'd see Ethan that night at book club, so I decided to head to the hospital to speak to Dr. Cutie Pie, the nickname I came up with for him pre-Zak. Ryder was a healer. I couldn't imagine him as a killer, but in my experience, a lot of people I would never have believed capable of doing such a horrendous thing had turned out to be murderers after all.

"Ryder in?" I asked the nurse at the front desk.

"He's in his office. You can go on back."

"Okay, thanks."

"No Charlie today?" the nurse asked.

"No. He's at home. I'm just popping in to ask a quick question."

"There's a six-year-old girl with us who would really benefit from Charlie's special brand of comforting if you have time to bring him by later."

"Absolutely. I'll bring him by right after lunch."

I headed down the hallway to Ryder's office. It had been a while since I'd brought Charlie by to do his therapy thing. I was going to have to make more of an effort. He provided a lot of comfort to those in pain. When Charlie and I had come up with the idea for him to serve as a therapy dog, it was Ryder Westlake who had made it happen.

"Hey, Zoe, where's your better half?" Ryder greeted me when I walked into his office.

"Charlie isn't with me now, but I'm going to bring him by after lunch. The reason I'm here is to ask about your Halloween costume."

"Yeah, about that. I'm afraid I'm not going to make it to your party as I had originally planned. The doctor who was supposed to be on duty that night had a family emergency and had to fly home, so I'm covering for him."

"I'm sorry to hear that. Maybe you can return your costume for a refund."

"Don't have to. I sold it to Benny Feldman last week."

I frowned. Benny? I couldn't believe he'd kill a man, but he'd been at the haunted house just a short time before I stumbled across the body, and if he had the black robe …

Chapter 11

I tried to track down Benny, but he wasn't at his job or his apartment. I considered just sharing what I knew with Lesserman, but I wasn't certain Benny was guilty of anything and I didn't want the deputy to start hassling him until I was sure.

When I got home from the hospital Zak had some interesting news that occupied the remainder of the morning.

"I've been looking into the possible link between Alvin and Isaac," Zak informed me. "It seems that Alvin and Isaac's father, George, were friends."

"Friends? Friends how?"

"Based on the information I could dig up, it looks as if they met in college. They both attended Oxford between 1883 and 1887. Alvin was the son of a duke, so a higher education was expected of him, and although George was a commoner, his father was a scholar who published several volumes about the history of the area where they lived."

"If Alvin was the son of a duke do we know why he was in Ashton Falls in 1915?" I asked.

"Not really. I found an old article that was published in a London newspaper that mentioned that Alvin was coming to America in 1895. He was thirty at the time. The article didn't say why he was coming or how long he planned to stay, and I can't find anything that explains what he was doing in a little mining town. It's possible his stay in Devil's Den was part of a different trip entirely. I'm still trying to find something that shows whether Alvin lived in America from 1895 until he died in 1915 or if he went back to England at some point after his 1895 trip and then returned in 1915."

I stood behind Zak, looking over his shoulder at his computer screen. He was toggling back and forth between the various documents he'd uncovered. I suppose if Alvin and George were friends and Alvin had a mission he needed to entrust to someone he knew he could depend on, he might call upon that friend's son. It still didn't explain what he could have had in his possession that was so important that he would ask a man to travel halfway across the globe to retrieve.

"Did you uncover anything that might indicate whether Alvin had a wife and children?"

"No, but I'll keep looking. I need to head over to the academy in an hour or so. I thought I'd grab some lunch. Care to join me?"

"I'd love to," I found myself saying, despite the candy bar and taco I'd already eaten that morning. "By the way, Tiffany is all set to watch the house and the animals over Thanksgiving, so I guess the ski trip is on."

Zak pulled me into his arms. "I love our life here, but I'm counting the days until I can have you all to myself."

I wound my arms around Zak's neck. "Yeah, me too. It'll be nice to sleep in and not have to worry about having a million things to take care of."

Zak kissed me on the lips. "And it will be nice to spend time in our private hot tub and not have to worry about getting kids to bed."

I looked into Zak's eyes. "So how hungry are you?"

"Suddenly, not at all. At least not for food."

After Zak and I had "lunch," Charlie and I headed to the hospital to visit the little girl. She was a tiny thing who looked lost in the big bed the hospital provided, with tubes and monitors attached to various parts of her body that Charlie and I would need to be careful not to disturb. I almost commanded Charlie to remain on the floor until I saw her whole face light up when Charlie jumped up onto the foot of her bed. I had him lie down next to the girl and then carefully arranged the equipment so it wouldn't be disturbed.

"What's his name?" the girl asked.

"Charlie. And I'm Zoe. What's your name?"

"Charisa."

"It looks like you have a lot of tubes for such a little girl."

The girl sighed. "The doctors keep doing tests, but they don't know what's wrong with me."

I frowned. "How long have you been sick?"

"A while. The doctors are trying to make me better, but it isn't working."

"I'm so sorry. I know how hard it is to be in the hospital."

"It's boring and the tests make me feel bad."

Charlie put a paw on the girl's stomach. She grinned. "Do you always come to the hospital?" she asked.

"Not always. I happened to stop by today and the nurse told me you needed some Charlie time."

"Oh, I do. Can he come again?"

"I'll speak to Dr. Westlake, but as long as it's okay with him, we'll definitely come again. Maybe even tomorrow if you're still here."

"I want to go home, but the doctors say I'm too sick. I don't like it here, but I don't want to go to another hospital either."

"They might move you?"

"Dr. Westlake wants to send me down the mountain to a big hospital with a special doctor, but my mom can't get off work to go with me and I don't want to go by myself."

"I can understand that. Tell me what you like to do when you aren't in the hospital."

Charisa and I talked for almost an hour before I realized I needed to leave. I spoke to Dr. Westlake, who confirmed that it would be fine for Charlie to come for another visit the next day. He also explained that Charisa needed to see a specialist, but the mother wouldn't permit her daughter to be moved unless she could go with her and her boss was refusing to allow her paid time off. Maybe

Zak and I could help in some way. If money was the only obstacle to getting Charisa the help she needed we would definitely do what we could.

By the time Charlie and I left the hospital it was time to pick Scooter up from school. He had soccer practice that afternoon, so there wouldn't be time to talk to Zak about Charisa's situation until later that evening.

"How was school?" I asked Scooter.

He grinned as he held up his spelling test, which had a giant *A* written on it in red ink.

"Awesome!" I raised my hand for a high-five.

"My teacher said she's proud of me."

"I'm proud of you too. We have soccer right now, but I think a congratulatory ice cream cone might be in order afterward."

Scooter clicked his seat belt across his lap. "Coach said he's going to make me and Tucker starting forwards. He said we're a force to be reckoned with."

I smiled. "You are at that. I'm glad Tucker decided to join the team. You work well together. I'm looking forward to the tournament in a couple of weeks."

"Coach said if we make it to the championships we'll play Thanksgiving week. I told him I wasn't going to be here and he said he was sorry to hear that."

"I imagine he was."

"Do I have to go to my grandparents'?"

I pulled into the parking lot near the soccer field. "I really think you do. Your grandparents love you. They miss you. I know you have a life here now and it's important to you, but your grandparents are your family. They want to spend time with you when they can and they haven't seen you for a long time."

"Yeah." Scooter sighed. "I know."

"Besides, your dad said he might be there. I know you'll want to see him if he's able to make it."

"He won't come. He never does."

I hated to admit it, but I was willing to bet Scooter was right. Dang those parents who let their kids down time after time. It really wasn't right.

"Grab your cleats. We don't want to be late," I instructed.

Soccer practice ran late, so by the time we got home it was time for me to leave again. Zak handed me a sandwich as I headed out the door. I thought about skipping book club, but I really did want to talk to Ethan. Not only was he one of the five men on the monk's robe list and I really wanted to get him crossed off but he was a historian who might be able to shed some light on why Alvin had been in Devil's Den in the first place.

Hazel had really outdone herself this evening. She presented a pleasant place for us to hold our meetings and consistently provided delicious snacks but in the spirit of Halloween, this week she'd gone all out with seasonal flower arrangements, scented candles, delicious and artfully presented appetizers, and holiday accents throughout.

"Your house looks amazing," I complimented Hazel.

"Thank you, dear. I'm pleased with the way it turned out. I wanted a seasonal feel without the gaudy."

I laughed. "Wait until you see our place. Zak has officially turned back into the overly obsessed Halloween decorator. Although I have to say the kids are feeding his frenzy. Especially Alex. I can't believe how many different kinds of Halloween decorations you can buy. Every time I come home there's a new mechanical monster or a blow-up figure in the yard."

Hazel smiled. "Zak does tend to go overboard in his enthusiasm, but I'm happy to see him acting like a kid for a change. Alex too. They both have a tendency to be a bit too serious."

"I guess that's true," I admitted. "I'm afraid Alex's habit of overthinking things has landed her in a bit of a predicament."

I explained about the situation she was facing with her mother and a trip she didn't want to take over the holidays.

"I'll think it over. I'm sure I can come up with something that even her parents will determine takes priority over a visit. Though I suspect convincing them might be easier than you think. It seems to me that they aren't all that excited about having her with them anyway."

I sighed. "So true. I imagine the invitation was a response to Alex's less-than-sincere e-mail stating that she was sad they wouldn't be together at Christmas. I bet they'll be relieved if Alex is tied up in Ashton Falls."

"I do feel bad for the poor girl. I'm glad she has you and Zak." Hazel picked up a serving tray with small bites of several delicious creations. "I'm going to pass these around before we begin."

"I need to speak to Ethan in private. Would it be okay to use your library?"

"Absolutely. I'll ask him to meet you there. If you pull him aside everyone is going to wonder why, and we both know that once the group gets onto the murder case we'll never get around to discussing the book."

"Thanks. I'll head back there now."

This wasn't the first time Hazel had helped me to separate those I needed to speak with from the crowd. I was sad that my grandma had passed and I missed her every day, but I didn't want Pappy to spend his remaining days alone, and if he couldn't be with Grandma, I would just as soon have him with Hazel. She was kind and intelligent and seemed to make him smile.

"You wanted to see me?" Ethan asked when he joined me in the library.

"Did you put on a monk's robe and kill Duncan?"

"What? Why would you even ask that?"

"You're on my list." I held up the paper.

"And how did you come up with this particular list?" Ethan asked.

I explained about the robe and my discovery that seven of them had been in stock and six had been sold and picked up.

"It looks like everyone is crossed off except Benny," Ethan observed.

"And you. Did you kill Duncan?"

"Of course not. I was at the Hamlet the entire evening. A lot of people saw me there."

I crossed Ethan's name off the list. "I didn't really think you did it, but in the movies it's always the person you least suspect."

Ethan frowned. "And are we thinking Benny killed Duncan?"

I shrugged. "His is the only name left on the list and he was at the haunted house that night. In fact, he left about thirty minutes before I did. I also know he was miffed at Duncan for trashing the place. I hate to think he would be driven to killing the man, but it does seem to add up."

"Have you spoken to him?" Ethan asked.

"Not yet. I looked for him today, but he wasn't at work or at his apartment. I guess I'll fill Lesserman in tomorrow. I didn't want to throw Benny's name into the mix if I wasn't sure he was guilty, but it's looking pretty damaging right now."

"I think sharing what you know with the deputy is a good move. What does Zak think?"

"I haven't actually asked him. He's been busy trying to figure out how the

Duke of Everlay and Isaac Wainwright are related."

"Who's the Duke of Everlay?"

I told Ethan everything I could remember about what Zak had discovered. I'd forgotten a few of the specifics like dates, but I thought I had a pretty good grasp on the situation.

"You say Isaac's father went to college with the duke's son?"

"That's what Zak said."

Ethan frowned. "I might know something, but I need to do some checking. The books I need are at my house. I'm game to skip the book discussion and pick this conversation back up at my place if you are."

"Let's go. The sooner I get this whole thing figured out the better."

Ethan's house looked exactly like you'd expect the home of a single male history professor who'd traveled the world would. The walls were lined with shelves that held books, art, and artifacts. The entire house was decorated in tones of brown and beige, and the furniture had been selected for comfort rather than aesthetic appeal.

Ethan's office featured a huge desk that was surrounded by file cabinets and bookshelves. The only softness to the room was the large fluffy white cat who watched us from the sofa.

I sat down on one of the leather chairs across from Ethan's desk while he walked around the room pulling books off shelves. He looked to be intent on his task and seemed to know what he was looking for, so I didn't offer to help.

After he had pulled four of five volumes he seemed happy with he returned to his desk. He opened the first book and began thumbing through it. He located what he was looking for at last, then passed the book across the desk. The page was open to a photo of two men.

"This," Ethan pointed to the man on the right, "is Alvin Everlay, and this," he indicated the other, "is Isaac Wainwright's father. The photo was taken when they were both attending university. It seems George ran out of funds to continue his studies, so the duke paid for the remainder of his education at the request of his son."

"Wow, so the men weren't just friends, they were *good* friends."

"For a while."

"They had a falling out?" I asked.

"They did." Ethan opened a different book and, as before, passed it across the desk. There was a wedding photo of George and his new bride.

"The falling-out occurred when George fell in love with Alvin's girl. It was pretty much unheard of for a woman to choose a nearly bankrupt commoner over the wealthy son of a duke, but she did. Her name was Evette."

"So this must be Isaac's mother."

"Yes. Evette and George had eleven children when all was said and done. Isaac was the eldest."

I frowned. "Okay, they were friends until George stole Alvin's girl. I'm assuming the friendship ceased to exist at that point. So why would Alvin leave whatever it was he left to Isaac?"

Ethan drummed his fingers on the desk as he considered the situation.

It was an odd set of circumstances that brought Isaac to the States. Unless…"I spoke to a man named Gus who was owed a large amount of money by Duncan," I informed Ethan. "He said Duncan had some sort of a plan to get the money. He mentioned an inheritance. What if Alvin and Evette had a fling behind George's back? He loved her, and maybe after she married George she regretted her decision. What if the fling ended in pregnancy?"

"Isaac," Ethan supplied. "Alvin and Evette know the truth, but Evette is married to George, and they realize that pursuing their relationship would end in heartache all around, so they keep the fact that Alvin is actually Isaac's father to themselves. Eventually, watching some other man raise his son becomes too much for him so he runs away and comes to America. On his deathbed he wants his son to know the truth, so he sends him the letter Duncan found. In the letter Alvin tells Isaac that he has left something for him in Devil's Den and gives him a set of encrypted instructions to find it."

I narrowed my gaze. "Yeah, but the part of the letter we found didn't say anything about Alvin being Isaac's father. It just stated that he left him something he wanted him to come to the States to retrieve. Of course it looks as if there must have been two or more pages to the letter and we only found the first one, so maybe the revelation of Isaac's parentage is on another page."

"Perhaps."

"The question is, why would Alvin want Isaac to come to America?" I asked. "Why not just mail him whatever it was he wanted him to have?"

"It does seem as if that would have been easier and more direct. Asking him to make this huge voyage seems unnecessary. And Alvin must have shared with him what it was he left him, and it must have been valuable; otherwise why would Isaac comply with the wishes of a man he'd never met?"

"The legend tells us that Isaac came to Devil's Den to search for a stone. Maybe it was a diamond or something even more valuable. I sure wish we had the rest of the letter."

"Maybe we should go back to the mine when it's light to have another look," Ethan suggested.

"I'm game if you are. Of course, even if we figure out what it was Alvin left for Isaac and what might have become of it, that doesn't necessarily explain why Duncan was killed all these years later. I mean, it's been a hundred years. Whatever it is Alvin left can't possibly still be on anyone's radar."

"I agree," Ethan commented. "It's doubtful the relationship between Alvin and Isaac plays into Duncan's death. If I were you, I'd look at other motives."

"I guess we're back to Benny."

Chapter 12

Friday, October 30

The Halloween spirit had most definitely gripped the entire Donovan-Zimmerman extended family. It was dress-up day at the elementary school Scooter attended, and he was proudly displaying his ninja costume. Alex had gotten into the spirit by wearing black pants and an orange sweater and Pi had on black pants and a black T-shirt with his black leather jacket. Zak was already outside stringing lights even though it was colder than heck and the sun had only just poked its head over the horizon. And I had joined in with the fun and dug out an old jack-o'-lantern sweatshirt I'd had since middle school. Yup, it still fit, which is a true testament to how tiny I really am.

"We only have a half day of school, so my classes are over at eleven," Alex reminded me as I spooned oatmeal into a bowl. "And Zimmerman Academy is closed, so I'll need a ride home."

"We're out early as well," Pi informed me.

"Me too," Scooter added.

So much for a morning of sleuthing.

"Okay, I'll pick everyone up in the usual places," I confirmed. "Given the tight schedule, I might be late picking one or more of you up, but I'll be there."

"Maybe we should get Pi a car," Alex suggested. "That way he can help with the driving."

"Yeah," Pi agreed. "Maybe we should get Pi a car."

"You don't have your driver's license yet," I said.

"I can get it. I'm sixteen and I've taken the class. Or at least I took the class that was required where I used to live. I guess I should check the requirements here."

"Let's talk to Zak about that after Halloween. Right now I doubt he'll be interested in any conversation where the subject matter isn't dead and doesn't suck blood."

"He does seem to be really into the whole decorating thing," Alex responded. "Is he always like this at Halloween?"

"I think last year was the first time the fever really hit him, but now that he has it I'd be willing to bet it'll be an annual thing."

I began getting out the ingredients for assembling the sack lunches Scooter and Alex took with them. Pi usually preferred to wait to eat until he was finished with school and could pick up fast food.

"Do you even have lunch today considering it's an early release day?" I asked the younger two.

"I do," Alex confirmed, "but it'll be so early I doubt I'll be hungry. Maybe I'll just take an apple."

"I do, too, but I don't need a lunch 'cause of the party. Do we have my punch and cupcakes?" Scooter asked.

Thanks to Zak, we did.

"And the goodie bags?"

"They're all packed and on the table near the entry. I even had extra spiders for each bag because Zak bought some, as well as some extra candy and some cool Halloween cards with coupons on them for a free ice cream at the parlor in town. "

"This is going to be the best Halloween ever." Scooter grinned.

I had to agree. I knew I was superexcited. There was just something about holidays and kids that seemed to go together.

I dropped everyone at school and decided to check in with Ellie. I'd been so busy that I hadn't so much as called her the previous day. She seemed to be doing better with Mariah, but I could see the situation was still really hard on her. When I arrived at the boathouse she was sitting on the back deck in tears.

"What happened?" I hugged my best friend as tight as I could.

"Skye," she sobbed.

My heart sank. It must be bad if Ellie was this upset. "Did she die?" I asked softly.

"No. She woke up."

I pulled back just a bit. Woke up? Wasn't that a good thing?

"Don't get me wrong." Ellie took a deep breath. "I'm so very happy and so very thankful that she's going to be okay. I really am. I've been so worried about her since the accident. It's just that…"

"Mariah," I realized. "It's hit you that she'll be going home."

"I know Mariah isn't mine and I really am happy that she can be with her mama, but…"

"Having her here reminded you what you're missing," I provided.

Ellie nodded her head.

"Oh, honey, I'm so sorry."

Ellie wiped her eyes with the back of her hand. I looked around for a tissue but didn't see one.

"I'm sure Skye will let you visit Mariah any time you want. After what happened maybe you'll even be close again."

"I'm sure Skye will let me visit. In fact, she's already suggested it. And while I'm happy I'll have the opportunity to renew my relationship with Skye and to have Mariah in my life, it isn't enough. I've decided I'm going to have the surgery that will increase my chances of having a successful pregnancy," Ellie informed me. "I've thought about it a lot this week. I'm not saying I'm going to run out and get pregnant right away, but I want to be ready when the time is right."

"You know I'm here for you. You know I'll do anything in my power to help you through this, but having a child is a big step."

"I know."

I sat down on one of the yard chairs Ellie had scattered around the deck. "Have you discussed this with Levi?"

"No. Not yet. I know my decision to pursue having a baby will spell the end of our relationship, and as mad as I am at the guy right now, I do love him and I'm not making this decision lightly. I know having the discussion with him I need to have will be emotionally draining and I don't think I can deal with that right now. I'm going to wait until after I take Mariah home and things settle down a bit. I may even wait until after the holidays. I thought I'd try to get an appointment with the fertility specialist I spoke to before, so I have all the information before I decide."

"I think that's a good idea."

"In the meantime I'm just going to enjoy the time I have left with Mariah. Now that she's gotten used to me we're really having a good time."

"Do you know when she'll be going home?" I asked.

"It'll be another week at least. I'm not really sure. I told Skye I'd bring Mariah for a visit, but she thinks it will be harder on the baby to see her and then have to leave again. Skye is dying to see her, but she wants what's best for Mariah. That's real love. That's the way love should be."

"Levi loves you." I knew she was comparing Levi's commitment to her with Skye's commitment to her baby.

"Maybe. But maybe that isn't enough. You know I've struggled with the fact that we just don't seem to have the level of commitment we should if we're going to pursue a long-term relationship."

"Yeah, I know."

I watched Ellie as she looked out across the lake. A myriad of emotions danced across her face as she appeared to watch a duck family as they glided across the glassy water. I supposed when you longed for a child, babies of any kind could tug at your heartstrings. I didn't need to watch Ellie's face to know how much she wanted to have a baby. And I knew what a good mom she would be. I really thought Ellie and Levi had a chance at the happily ever after Zak and I shared, but I also knew this conflict could make that future impossible.

I hugged Ellie again. "You know I'll always be here for you. I love you."

"I love you too."

After I left the boathouse I headed out to look for Benny. He was the only person I still had on my monk's costume list, other than the person who'd paid cash and was therefore untraceable. I didn't know Benny really well, but he was a nice guy and I found myself hoping he would prove to be innocent. Of course, if the killer was the unidentifiable person who'd bought the last costume I didn't know how I'd ever find him.

Benny was an electrician by trade. I stopped by his shop but was told he was out on a call. I kind of knew the clerk, who was willing to give me the address of the place he was working that morning. I didn't have a lot of time before I had to pick up Alex, who was the first of the three kids to get out of school that day, but I figured I wouldn't need a lot to find out if Benny was the man I'd seen in the cemetery.

"It was me," Benny said when I confronted him as he rewired an old cabin near the lake.

"You killed Duncan Wright?"

"What? No! You asked me if it was me you saw in the cemetery the night of the haunted house. It was me, but I didn't kill the guy."

I took a deep breath. "Maybe you should start at the beginning."

"After I said good-bye to you, I went out to my car. When I got there I saw another car parked on the road near mine. I realized it belonged to Duncan. I had a feeling he'd come back to mess up what we had just finished cleaning. That made me mad. Really mad."

"Wait. You said his car was parked near yours? I don't remember seeing any cars other than my own when I went to the parking lot."

"I was parked on the old dirt road that runs behind the cemetery. So was Duncan."

"Why did you park there?" I wondered.

"I had all the sound equipment, so I wanted to park as close to the house as I could get without actually disturbing the cemetery or the decorations we'd set out. The road directly behind the house proved to have the closest entry point."

"Okay, I guess that makes sense; go on."

"Like I said, I was really mad when I saw Duncan's car. I had my monk's costume on my backseat, so I got the idea of scaring him. I hoped if he thought the place was haunted, like a lot of folks around here believe, he might stay away once and for all."

"So you tried to scare him, but he came after you, so you killed him?" I speculated.

"No. I told you, I didn't kill him. I never even saw him. At least not until you tripped over him. I was walking toward the house from the back of the cemetery when I saw you walking to your car. I noticed you saw me and began walking toward me. Initially, I was going to try to sneak away, but I didn't want to leave you wondering if you'd seen a ghost, so I turned around and walked back toward you. Before I could say anything you screamed and tripped over Duncan."

"Why didn't you help me? Or at the very least reveal who you were?"

"Once I saw Duncan was dead I figured you'd think I'd killed him."

Benny had a point. That was exactly what I would have thought. In a way, that was what I still thought. He had a story, but he didn't have an alibi.

"After I realized what you'd tripped over I panicked and ran," Benny continued.

I narrowed my gaze. "If that's true where's Duncan's car now?"

"I don't know. I swear. After you tripped over the body, I didn't wait to find out what was going to happen. I just left. When I went back the next day after they canceled the haunted house the car was gone. Maybe the deputy took it."

"Maybe. I guess I'll have to ask him."

Benny began to squirm. I could see our conversation was making him nervous. "You do believe me, don't you?"

"I'm not sure," I answered truthfully. "But at this point I'm going to give you the benefit of the doubt."

Benny looked relieved.

"Did you see anyone else other than me that night?"

Benny paused, I assumed, to consider my question.

"Even for a minute," I added. "Maybe a shadow?"

"Actually, I did see someone. A large man wearing dark clothing. He was pretty far away, so I couldn't see his face. I bet he was the killer. Damn, I wish I'd thought of this earlier. I bet the guy is long gone by now."

"Can you think of anything at all that might help me track the guy down? Even a minor detail could help."

"Like I said, it was dark, and at the time I didn't suspect anything was wrong, so I didn't pay that much attention, but I'm pretty sure the guy had a limp."

Something about Benny's statement wasn't adding up, but I wasn't entirely certain what it was. Still, my Zodar was tingling, and as far as I was concerned, that was proof enough that all was not quite as Benny wanted me to believe.

Chapter 13

I picked the kids up from school and dropped them at the house, then decided maybe it was time for me to have another chat with Lesserman. I didn't like the guy, but I was interested in what, if anything, he'd managed to discover, as well as whether he'd found Duncan's car. I couldn't believe I actually missed Salinger, but I did. I hoped his cruise wasn't going to be a long one. I was pretty sure he was halfway to nowhere when I'd spoken to him.

"Hey, Janice. I've come to speak to the beast. Is he around?"

"Salinger is still on vacation. I don't expect him back for another week."

"Actually," I clarified, "that wasn't the beast I was referring to. I've come to speak to Lesserman."

"I'm afraid he isn't here either. I expect him back in a couple of hours if you want to check back. Fair warning, though: he still thinks you're a prime suspect in Duncan Wright's murder. I know there have been several people who have vouched for you, including me, but his mind seems to be made up."

"What a waste." I sighed. "If he thinks I'm the killer I doubt he's looking very hard for the person who actually did it."

"Yeah, I suppose that's true to a point, but I will say he's actually been working on the case."

"Can you at least tell me if he's recovered Duncan's car?"

Janice hesitated.

"Come on. You know I didn't do it, and you know I have the best shot at solving this in Salinger's absence."

"No car," Janice said. "They didn't find it at the scene and they didn't find it anywhere else either. Lesserman thinks maybe Duncan arrived at the graveyard with someone who used the car to leave the scene of the murder after he was killed."

I frowned. "Based on the account of a source, the car was still there for some time after Duncan was most likely murdered."

Janice shrugged. "I don't know. That's just what Lesserman came up with. How reliable is your source?"

"Not very," I admitted.

"If you talk to Lesserman please don't bring up the car thing. He'll most likely assume I told you about the car and I don't want to lose my job."

"Don't worry, I won't tell. Do you know if Lesserman has searched the mine site?"

"I know he was up there, but I don't think he found anything. Not that he tells me every single detail, but the guy hates to type, so he has me handle the daily reports on his progress that he's sending to the main office."

I realized Lesserman's laziness might work out well for me if I could keep Janice talking.

"When I was up there I saw the yellow caution tape wrapped around the trailer. I also noticed the interior of the trailer was trashed. Do you happen to know if that happened before Lesserman found it, or did he trash it himself, looking for clues?"

"It was already trashed. His notes indicate it was obvious that someone was there looking for something."

"Did he speculate whether he thought they found what they were looking for?"

"He didn't say."

"Do you have any reason to believe Lesserman might go up to the mine site this afternoon?"

"You're going to go snoop," Janice accused me.

"Not snoop. Just look around."

"Looking around is snooping, but no, I don't think he'll be up at the mine site today. I think he figures he's learned as much as he can about what may or may not have happened from the site."

I smiled my friendliest smile. "I know it's your job to keep things confidential. And I do appreciate your sharing information with me. I promise I won't mention any part of our conversation to Deputy Clueless."

Janice tried not to smile, but I could see she was fighting the urge.

"I do have one more tiny little question and then I promise I'll leave you alone."

"What?" Janice asked warily.

"Do you know if Lesserman has any pages that might come from a very old letter in evidence?"

Janice frowned. "A letter?"

"I found the first page of a letter Duncan had that was written over a hundred years ago. It seems there were additional pages I didn't find. I thought they might have been on his person when he was murdered."

Janice logged onto her computer, then pulled up a file. She squinted her eyes as she considered the information in front of her. "I don't see a mention of a letter or any other type of correspondence."

"Okay, thanks. Have a wonderful rest of your day."

I left the sheriff's office and headed toward the mine. I remembered Ethan expressing interest in looking around there, but I had a busy evening and didn't want to waste time tracking him down. Besides, I didn't plan to spend a lot of time up there myself. If Lesserman was done with the place, I reasoned, there couldn't be any harm in my looking at the interior of the trailer. I sort of doubted I'd find anything, but it couldn't hurt to look for myself.

I should have turned around and headed home the minute I saw the car parked behind the trailer. I didn't recognize the vehicle, but if there was someone else at the mine chances were they were up to no good. Of course, my totally illogical Zoe logic allowed me to convince myself that the car must belong to someone else who was curious about what Duncan had been doing up here on the hill.

After I parked I looked around. I didn't see anyone, so I decided to look in the trailer and then head home. A quick glance through the open doorway gave evidence to the fact that no one had been by to clean up the mess that had been left by the prowler. I noticed broken glass on the floor, so I took Charlie back to wait in the car. No use risking an injury to his little paws.

I didn't really know what I was looking for, but I guess I figured when I saw it I would recognize it. I sort of hoped to find the missing page or pages to the letter, but even I realized that was asking for a lot. Duncan was an unpopular man who seemed to have made a lot of enemies. Maybe I'd find evidence of someone sending him threatening letters. But the only thing I found that seemed important at all was a stack of keno cards from a casino two states away. I sort of doubted it was relevant to the current case, but it did seem to lend support to the fact that Duncan had a gambling problem.

The man sure had accumulated a lot of junk considering he'd only been in the area for three weeks. And when had he had time to go to the casino? I supposed it was a short flight, but it seemed like quite an extravagance to travel that distance for an overnight trip. I didn't know much about gambling addictions, but I supposed a true addict would do what he needed to do to get his fix.

I stood in the center of the trailer and looked around. I'd really hoped to find something a bit more relevant. Of course Duncan had hidden the letter and other items I'd found, so the chances of him leaving anything important in the trailer had been slim to none. I was about to give up and go home when I heard a noise behind me. I turned to find a man standing in the doorway.

"What are you doing here?" I asked.

"I was about to ask you the same thing."

"I told you when we spoke before. Sometimes I do research for the sheriff's office. That's what I'm doing now. Research. That still doesn't tell me what you're doing here. You know this is a crime scene."

"You here by yourself?" the man asked.

I thought of Charlie. "No, I'm here with my partner."

The man looked around. "Don't see no partner."

"He's up in the mine." I needed to gain control of this situation and fast. "I'm afraid I'm going to have to ask you to leave. This is private property."

The man glared at me. "I'm not going anywhere. I'm looking for the gold mine, and I'm willing to bet that's what you're really doing here as well."

I frowned. "What gold mine? The old mine has been dried up for years."

"Not according to Duncan. He said he had a map to a gold mine. When I realized he was staying up here I figured this was where he found the gold."

I paused as I tried to make sense of what Gus was telling me. "The mine Duncan was referring to wasn't an actual gold mine," I explained. "He just used the term to indicate that he believed he was coming into some money."

"Yeah, he tried telling me that story too," Gus growled. "He thought he'd convince me that the fortune he was after was in the old cemetery. He even got me to go to the cemetery to look for it. He said once he found what he was looking for he would have plenty of money to pay me and everyone else back. But when we got to the cemetery and followed the clues they just led to a tombstone, not a treasure."

"A tombstone? Do you know which tombstone?"

"I was too mad to ask."

"So you killed him," I realized.

"The man had been stringing me along for months. I should have killed him, but I didn't. Still, I might need to kill you if I don't want everyone finding out about the gold mine."

"There is no gold mine," I shouted.

How dumb was this guy? When I noticed he had a gun I realized that wasn't the most important question of the moment.

"Look, I don't want the gold. Honest. My husband is a zillionaire. I don't need the money."

The man grinned. A really sick, crooked-tooth grin that, combined with his thin, pale face, made him look like a real monster.

"Nice try, but you aren't going anywhere."

"Are you going to shoot me?"

"No. I have a better idea."

Once I realized Gus's better idea involved my being locked in a dark, airtight room that had been used as a safe when the old mine was operational, I found myself wishing he'd just shot me. The idea of slowly suffocating to death in an airless chamber terrified me more than I could say. I began to sob as I heard the man's car pull away. There was no way anyone was going to find me before the oxygen in my tomb ran out.

I needed to try to calm down. To stop hyperventilating. I was using the available air at twice the necessary rate. I closed my eyes so I wouldn't realize how dark it was and tried to think calming thoughts.

The party the following night with all my friends and family. I really had been looking forward to that. And my romantic trip with Zak. He was going to be devastated. And Charlie. He wouldn't understand why I'd left him in the car and never come back.

I wiped the tears that were steaming down my face with the back of my hand. Thinking of those I loved and would leave behind was too painful. It would be better not to think at all. I tried to shut off my mind and shallow my breath. I'd read somewhere that yogis could live for days with very little air. Maybe someone would find me if I could hang on for days rather than hours.

I'm not sure how much time passed. There was no way to gauge the minutes as they turned to hours. I felt myself begin to drift off as my breath became labored. I was on the verge of giving in to the darkness when I heard cars pulling up outside. I tried to yell, but I didn't have the strength.

I closed my eyes and began to sob when I heard the shots. I was sure that, once again, Zak had come to my rescue, but this time he'd gotten himself killed for his efforts. I'd thought Gus had left, but he must have returned. If Zak was dead I didn't want to live. Part of me wanted to give in to the urge to gasp the last of the air, but I thought of those who would mourn me. I used the last of my strength to pound on the door.

I began to black out as I heard a noise on the other side of the door. I looked up as a loud explosion accompanied the opening of the door. I took a deep breath and began to sob when the last person I expected to see crashing into the room appeared. He ran forward and gathered me in his arms. He carried me out into the fresh air.

"What are you doing here?" I sobbed.

"I couldn't very well let anything happen to my lucky charm, now could I?"

"I bet you were surprised to see Salinger's face when he came crashing through the door," Levi joked later that evening, after everyone had gathered to finish preparing for the party.

"I couldn't have been any more surprised if it was the Loch Ness monster that came to rescue me."

"It was actually really sweet of him to cut his cruise short and fly home," Ellie added.

"It *was* sweet and I'm very grateful. I even invited him to the party tomorrow when I was finished sobbing, but he thought that might be pushing the friendship thing a little far."

"How did he know where to find you?" Ellie asked.

"I told Janice I wanted to check out the old mine and she mentioned it to Salinger when he showed up at the office. I'm glad he realized I'd made a mess of things and came after me right away. If he hadn't I wouldn't have made it out alive."

I stood on tiptoe to string orange lights around the banister. We already had white lights there, but Zak had decided we needed orange as well. To be honest, I think his last-minute decorating frenzy is his way of dealing with the fact that I almost died. Again. He was pretty upset I'd gone out to the mine without telling him what I was doing, and I'd had to promise like a million times that from now on I'd bring him with me whenever I went sleuthing.

Of course, if he had been with me, he wouldn't have had a gun, so we would most likely both have ended up in the airless room. With two of us breathing we would have lasted half the time and would most likely both be dead. I decided not to point that out, however, because he probably realized that, and my little near-death experience really had shaken him up.

"So you figured out who scared you in the graveyard and who killed Duncan, but did you ever figure out what Duncan was after?" Levi asked.

"Maybe. Gus said he came to Ashton Falls because Duncan had mentioned a gold mine. I realized it was a metaphorical gold mine and not an actual one. Gus said Duncan led him to the cemetery and told him the secret to getting what he needed to pay him back was a tombstone. Gus didn't remember which one, but Duncan's body was found lying across Isaac Wainwright's grave, so I'm betting it was his tombstone Duncan was there to look at. Zak and I are going to go over to the graveyard to look at the headstone first thing in the morning. Do you guys want to come along?"

"Heck yeah," Levi answered.

Interactive Reader Portal: If you're reading the story chronologically, read chapter 6 of *Zimmerman Academy* now and then return to the top of chapter 14. If you're reading *Zimmerman Academy* as a separate story, continue on to Chapter 14.

Chapter 14

Halloween

It had been a while since Zak, Levi, Ellie, and I had all been out sleuthing together, and I found I rather missed it. Things had changed since Zak and I had gotten married and taken on the Academy and the kids. I won't say things are better or worse than they were, but they're definitely different. For one thing, I spend a lot more time being a wife and surrogate mother than I do being a best friend. Maybe that was the way of life as you matured and took on adult responsibilities, but I did miss the *us* we used to be, so perhaps I needed to find a way to create a little better balance in my life.

"Isaac's headstone is over there." I pointed across the cemetery.

We covered the distance silently, each lost in our own thoughts.

"So what now?" Levi asked as we stood near the headstone. There didn't appear to be any secret compartments. At least not any that were visible.

"I don't know. Gus just said Duncan led him to the headstone, and that it held a secret that would bring him enough money to pay everyone back."

"Wait a minute," Zak said. "The legend states that Isaac came to the area to find a stone."

"Yeah. Which is why I'm thinking headstone," I answered.

"But Isaac's headstone didn't exist when Isaac was alive," Zak pointed out. "If Alvin did indeed want Isaac to find a headstone it would most likely be his own."

I rolled my eyes. Of course. Isaac hadn't been sent to find his own tombstone. Maybe I really was losing it.

"Do we know where Alvin is buried?" Levi asked.

"No," I said, "but the letter led us to this cemetery, so I'm going to go out on a limb and say he's buried here."

"Are we sure we're looking for a headstone?" Ellie asked.

"No, I'm not sure. I guess I just assumed that, as did Duncan, after the clues in the letter led us to this spot."

I looked around the area. The gravesites were over a hundred years old. Many were decayed, while others were gone altogether. Still, headstones were made of stone and, as the legend suggested, if we assumed Isaac did come to America to find a stone, it might have endured. We decided to each take our own row to see if we could find evidence of him having been buried in this cemetery.

We didn't.

I looked toward the house. It had been there when Isaac arrived in the area. I remembered Analee saying she suspected one of the reasons Duncan volunteered to help out with the Haunted Hamlet was because he wanted to have access to the house.

"What if the stone Isaac was sent to find was actually connected to the house rather than the cemetery?" I asked.

"Like a stone from the old fireplace?" Levi suggested.

"Or one of the stones from the patio," Ellie added.

"Yeah, something like that. Let's go take a look," I said. "Even if Duncan found what he was looking for, maybe we can figure out the clue."

The house actually had a lot of stone features, but I wasn't certain which were original to the house and which had been added later.

"Do we have any idea what we're looking for?" Ellie asked.

"Not really," I answered. "I guess if you find anything that looks significant give a holler."

We decided to split up and look around different parts of the house. I took the kitchen. I'm not sure why, but I had an intuition that the kitchen was the key to this whole mystery. I looked around the now tidy room. I thought about the fact that it had been a cleaver that had been used as a murder weapon. The cleaver had been inside the house earlier that day. I'd been operating under the assumption that Gus had lied and really had killed Duncan, but when would he have picked up the cleaver? He'd told me he'd come to the cemetery with Duncan, who'd promised him cash. When they arrived Duncan led him to Isaac's grave. The thing was, at no time did Gus mention going into the house. Of course he could have omitted that fact to throw me off, but if he'd planned to leave me for dead why bother to lie to me?

The only thing that made any sense was that Gus wasn't the killer. But if Gus wasn't the killer, who was? Usually when I'm really stumped during an investigation I find myself relying on the classic motives: love and money. Duncan owed

Gus money, but if he didn't do it that just left...

"Oh my God," I blurted out. "I know who did it. Gus didn't kill Duncan."

I ran into the living room. "I know who killed Duncan," I yelled.

Levi returned to the room. "I thought we decided Gus killed Duncan."

"We did, but we were wrong. I didn't stop to think about the cleaver. Duncan was killed with a cleaver that was in the kitchen. If Gus followed Duncan to the gravesite and killed him when Duncan failed to come up with the money, when did he get the cleaver?"

"What's all the yelling about?" Ellie asked as she came down the stairs with Zak on her heels.

"Zoe doesn't think Gus killed Duncan after all," Levi supplied.

"Then who did?" Ellie asked.

"Duncan's girlfriend, Analee," I said.

Zak frowned. "How do you figure that?"

"When I spoke to Analee she said Duncan had promised her that he would take her away to live somewhere tropical after he found the money he was looking for. When I found the box it contained a single airline ticket to Rio. My guess is that Analee found out Duncan planned to leave without her and came to the house to confront him. Analee mentioned to me that Duncan had wanted access to the house to look for something, so it makes sense she would look for Duncan here. My guess is they fought and she killed him in the heat of the moment. I'm going to assume she trashed the place to cover up what she'd done."

"That also explains the red paint," Levi pointed out. "She hoped it would cover up the blood."

"If Analee killed Duncan in the house how did the body get out to the graveyard?" Ellie asked.

"I'm not sure," I admitted. "Analee was a tiny little thing, but maybe she had help moving the body. Benny said Duncan came by while he was at the house on the day of the murder. He said he left Duncan to lock up. What if he didn't actually leave? Benny hated Duncan and he loved the event, so it seemed odd that he'd leave him in the house alone. It makes sense that Benny would hang around until after Duncan left. What if he witnessed the fight between Duncan and Analee? He might have helped her move the body." I turned to Levi. "When you arrived on Friday who else was here?"

"Just Benny. Why?"

"What was Benny doing?"

Levi paused. "He was messing around with something up in the attic."

"Did you go up there yourself?" I asked.

"No. I just saw that the little trapdoor was open, so I called up to let him know I was here. He came down then. To be honest, I didn't think anything about it. Why? Is it important?"

"I don't know. Maybe. See if you can find a ladder. I want to have a look to see if I can figure out what Benny was doing up there."

Levi found a ladder and I climbed up to the attic and was able to answer at least part of the question. Alvin's headstone was there, lying on its side. If you looked at the part that would usually be buried in the dirt a small compartment was visible, and it was clearly empty.

"Guess we're too late for the treasure," Levi stated the obvious.

"Guess so." I found I was disappointed at the anticlimax. "I suppose all we can do now is call Salinger. If Analee was here maybe he can find fingerprints or traces of DNA. We know Benny was here, and if he did help her maybe he'll crack if Salinger brings him in for questioning."

Chapter 15

"Benny confessed to everything," I informed Ethan, Phyllis, and Will Danner, our new math teacher, that evening when they arrived for the party. Will had come dressed as a monk, wearing, I assumed, the seventh, unaccounted-for costume. I was glad we'd figured everything out before I knew he had that costume. I'd have hated to suspect him.

"It went down pretty much like I'd thought. Benny said he knew the headstone was in the attic. He found it when he went up there to run some wiring for the sound system. He didn't know how it got there because the thing is heavy, but he knew the legend, so he spent a good amount of time looking for some sort of a clue."

"So he was in the attic when Duncan showed up," Ethan realized.

"Yep. He wasn't sure Duncan knew about the headstone so he kept quiet. Duncan appeared to be looking for something until Analee showed up and confronted him about not taking her with him to Rio. They fought and he struck her.

She picked up the cleaver and hit him with it."

Phyllis grimaced. "What an unpleasant way to die."

"Yeah," I agreed, although I might take that over slowly suffocating. "Anyway, Analee panicked when she realized what she'd done. In fact, she had a total meltdown. Benny felt bad for her, so he went downstairs and offered to help."

"They moved the body," Will said.

I nodded. "They moved it into the cemetery. Benny realized he'd need to find a more permanent hiding place, but he also knew the haunted house crew would be coming at any minute, so he decided to set the body out of the way and then come back later, after everyone had gone. Benny happened to have red paint in his car, which he realized would help mask the blood, so he and Analee spread it around and then trashed the place so it would look like vandalism. After everyone had gone Benny went back to move the body. He got the idea of using the monk's robe to disguise his identity just in case. He thought I'd left, but I'd taken longer to lock up than he predicted, so I saw him as he made his way toward the body. The rest you know."

"And the item Alvin left for Isaac?" Phyllis asked.

"I'm afraid I don't know."

"I might be able to shed some light on that," Ethan offered. "After we spoke I did some more research. I discovered Alvin had a very valuable stone: a red diamond worth tens of millions of dollars on today's market."

"Duncan found a diamond worth tens of millions of dollars?" I asked.

"No. If you look at historical records it seems Isaac's family did quite well financially after his death. It's my guess Isaac found the stone and sent it home before he was killed. Because the stone wasn't in his possession at the time of his death most people assumed he never found what he was looking for and the legend took hold."

"If it could be shipped why didn't Alvin send it in the first place?" I asked.

"I don't know. I don't suppose we ever will."

"So Duncan wasn't rich, he was just running away?" I thought of the plane ticket.

"It would seem so," Ethan answered. "As you said, he owed a lot of money to a lot of people."

I went in search of my parents and my adorable little sister. My mom, along with Ellie and Mariah, and Jeremy and Morgan, were in the den. Pepper and her boyfriend of sorts, Chad Carson, were sitting on the floor with the babies, making silly faces that caused them all to laugh hysterically. Ellie really was in her element among the babies. I knew how very much she wanted a child of her own, and in that moment I felt a conviction that she should have one. I hadn't always supported the baby idea, but from this point forward I intended to do just that.

"Is it okay if Eve and I go up to my room?" Alex asked as she walked up behind me. "We're working on a project for the Academy."

"Sure, that's fine. Have you seen Scooter?"

"He's in the pool with Tucker, Pi, and a few of the guys from the band."

One of the best things about the house was the year-round pool that could convert from indoor to outdoor as the weather dictated.

I headed back down the stairs, looking for Zak. We'd both been so busy lately that we'd barely had any time to connect.

"Are you having fun?" My dad walked up beside me, holding Harper in his arms.

"I am. In fact, I think this may be the best Halloween spooktacular I've ever thrown."

"I think you might be right. Have you seen your mom?"

"She's upstairs."

"I guess I should go up and get her. I think Harper has had enough Halloween fun for one night."

I reached for my sister, who was all but asleep. "I'll hold Harper while you get your stuff together. How was trick-or-treating?"

"It was fun. Harper was the cutest little Piglet out there. It was so fun to watch her hold her bag out for candy when each door was opened. And when each piece was dropped inside, she looked thrilled and amazed. Every single time."

I looked down at the toddler in my arms. "I'm sorry I missed it. Harper is growing up so fast. I've been so busy that I feel like I barely see her any more. I don't want to miss all the special baby moments."

"You'll have your own babies soon enough and they'll have their own special baby moments," my dad assured me.

"Yeah," I said as he turned to go. "I guess."

I smiled as Harper rested her head on my shoulder. The poor baby was exhausted. I loved the way her curly hair brushed my cheek as I held her. I did want to have Zak's baby one day; I just hoped the addition of children to the crazy life we already had wouldn't take away from the connection we now shared. There were times I was afraid the bond we felt as a newly married couple would fade and we would become strangers passing in the night as we juggled kids, jobs, and after-school activities.

I looked around the crowded room for Zak, but I didn't see him, so I headed for the pool. There, I found my totally awesome husband standing in the shallow end, waist deep in water, with both Scooter and Tucker hanging on him.

I looked at him and smiled. Our eyes locked and the noise in the room faded away. I knew now that, in spite of the baby in my arms and the preteens climbing on Zak's back, we were totally alone, even if we were alone in a room full of people. Maybe our love would survive the challenges I knew were ahead. Maybe Zak and I would beat the odds and our love would find a way. Maybe the secret to love everlasting can be found in the silence that bonded hearts share in the midst of chaos.

Zimmerman Academy

From the Diary of Phyllis King

Chapters 1 – 3 of Zimmerman Academy are included in the back of Hopscotch Homicide.

Chapter 4

Sunday, October 25

New Traditions

I have experienced many firsts since Brooklyn, Eve, and Pepper came to live with me. In many ways, I feel as if I am beginning a new chapter in my life at the ripe old age of sixty-two. In the past six weeks I have shared a home with someone other than my parents for the first time, gone on my first date, purchased and worn my first pair of jeans, and learned how to style my hair and apply makeup to bring out my best features. The first I am the most excited about, however, is sharing my first holiday with my new family. In the past I've never much bothered with the trappings associated with Halloween, or any other holiday, for that matter, but this year I want to establish new traditions and experience everything the season has to offer.

"Jeremy is here," Pepper called from downstairs.

"I'll be right down," I called back.

Jeremy Fisher is the assistant to my good friend Zoe Donovan. When I found out that he was going to be a single dad, I offered to let him rent one of the townhomes I own at a very reasonable price. At the time I thought I was doing the young man and his adorable daughter a favor, but Jeremy has allowed me to serve as a surrogate grandma to Morgan Rose, which has turned out to be a blessing without measure.

The girls absolutely adore Morgan, who is now eighteen months old, and she in turn adores them. Today we are babysitting Morgan while Jeremy is busy with his band. They are playing a concert in the park, which the girls and I plan to attend after we take Morgan shopping for her Halloween costume. The girls and I will be looking for costumes as well because we are all invited to a party at Zak and Zoe's home on Halloween night. As odd as it may sound, this will be my first Halloween costume ever.

"P'ma," Morgan greeted me as I walked into the room. When Morgan began to talk I couldn't decide what to have her call me. I wasn't her actual grandmother, so Grandma seemed presumptuous, but Phyllis, Ms. King, or Professor all seemed wrong as well. P'ma, an amalgamation of Phyllis and grandma, is the name we came up with after trial and error.

"How's my girl?" I asked as Morgan reached for me and I took her into my arms. Morgan is an adorable child with dark brown hair and huge brown eyes. The lashes that framed her eyes were long and thick.

"Kitty," Morgan said after she planted a wet kiss on my cheek.

"The kitty is upstairs," I answered. Surprisingly, my cat Charlotte, who doesn't like anyone, likes Morgan, and the two have formed a bond that I have to admit I don't completely understand.

"Cookie?" Morgan tried instead.

"How about if Pepper gets you a cookie while I talk to Daddy?" I set Morgan on the floor. "Be sure to put a bib on her so she doesn't get the cookie all over her pretty pink jumper."

"I will," Pepper assured me as she took Morgan's hand and led her into the kitchen, where I kept a supply of cookies made especially for toddlers.

"I really appreciate your doing this," Jeremy said.

"You know I love to spend the day with Morgan as often as I can," I answered. "The girls and I are going to do some shopping and then we will see you at the park. Did you have a specific theme in mind for Morgan's costume?"

"Whatever you decide will be fine. I'm just happy for the help. Zoe has been superbusy lately, which means she hasn't been spending much time at the Zoo, which translates into Tiffany and me putting in extra hours."

Tiffany Middleton was Zoe's other full-time employee besides Jeremy, who was actually the manager of the facility.

"Maybe Zoe should consider hiring some extra help," I suggested.

"We've talked about it, but she seems to think that once things settle down a bit she'll have more time to spend with the animals. The problem is that Zoe seems to have a knack for getting involved. In *everything*. I really don't see her freeing up much time in the near future, although it does slow down at the Zoo over the winter, after the bears go into hibernation and the snow discourages pets from wandering too far away from home. I think we'll be fine until spring."

"I know Zoe wants what is best for the animals, so if you do find you need extra help I definitely think you should bring it up again."

"I will." Jeremy looked at his watch. "I really should get going. I'll see you at the park. Have fun shopping."

Jeremy left and I headed toward the kitchen, where I could hear Pepper and Morgan laughing. Of the three young women who have come to live with me, Pepper is the most outgoing. Pepper is a fourteen-year-old with a kind heart and a whole lot of energy. She is also by far the least complicated and easiest to get along with of the three, an extreme extrovert who would generate enough energy to power a small town if we could figure out a way to harvest it.

I had to smile as I observed Pepper chatting with Morgan, who sat contentedly in her high chair with cookie smeared all over her face. The pair seemed to be having a good time, so I decided to head back upstairs to finish getting ready.

"Can we stop off at the health food store while we're in town?" Fifteen-year-old Eve asked as I passed her on the stairs.

"Absolutely. We can make any stops you girls want."

"Thanks. We're out of flax seed and granola. I meant to add them to the shopping list, but I forgot. We could probably use some more fruit and veggies for my shakes too, if we have time to go by the farmers market, and I overheard Brooklyn saying we were getting low on coffee."

"Not a problem. We'll pick everything up while we are out."

Eve is not only a vegetarian and a health food nut but she is an introvert like I am. She loves to read and I suspect she is secretly trying her hand at writing as well. In spite of the five-year age difference between them, she has a lot in common with Alex, and the two spend a lot of time working on a project neither of them seems willing to share. I asked Zoe about it, but she said Alex is being as secretive as Eve. If I didn't know the two girls so well I'd be worried, but if there was anyone you could trust to do the right thing it was Alex.

After I finished applying my makeup the way the girls had shown me, I braided my hair and grabbed the new leather jacket I'd splurged on. It is a deep caramel color that perfectly matches the leather boots I'd also decided to buy. I had to admit the jacket spoke to a wild side I never even knew I had.

I said good-bye to Charlotte and headed down the hall to knock on Brooklyn's door. She is a sixteen-year-old with a troubled past who I was certain I'd never be able to handle, but as it turns out, she is an agreeable girl with a willingness to take on the role of big sister to the others. We haven't discussed her need for the birth control pills she mentioned on her first day with me, but I do know she has been to the doctor in spite of the fact that she doesn't appear to have a steady boyfriend.

"Come in," Brooklyn called.

I opened the door halfway. "I just wanted to let you know we will be heading into town in a few minutes."

"Does this top make me look fat?"

"Fat?" I asked. Brooklyn watches her weight more religiously than anyone I've ever met. "I doubt any top could do that, but in answer to your question, the sweater is adorable and it absolutely does not make you look fat."

Brooklyn smiled. "Good. Pi said we might hang after the concert and I want to look my best."

"You look beautiful as always and I love that deep blue color on you. It accentuates your blond hair and blue eyes. You look just perfect, although you might want to grab a jacket if you plan to go out after the concert. The temperature here drops dramatically after the sun sets."

Brooklyn sighed as she opened her closet and looked at the options. "I need something new. Something different. Like the jacket you're wearing. It's the bomb, by the way."

Brooklyn was a diva who usually thinks my clothes need updating, so it tickled me to death that she actually wanted a jacket like mine.

"You can borrow it if you'd like," I offered.

Brooklyn grinned. "Really? You wouldn't mind?"

"Not at all." Secretly, I was thrilled that young, sophisticated Brooklyn would want to borrow *anything* of mine.

"That would be awesome. I'll take really good care of it. I promise."

I handed the garment to the teenager. "I know you will. We leave in fifteen minutes. I'll meet you downstairs."

After I checked in on Pepper and Morgan, I headed out to the garage to warm up the car. Today we would take the Volvo because we have Morgan with us, but on most weekends I prefer the Caddy convertible my daddy left to me. There is something about cruising along the highway with the radio blaring and the wind in your hair that frees up your inhibitions.

I've been giving a lot of thought to the costume I will look for. On one hand, I wouldn't feel comfortable with anything too extravagant or revealing. Brooklyn mentioned her intention to dress as Cleopatra, which I'm most certain she can pull off in spite of her blond hair, but I think a sixty-two-year-old virgin should dress a bit more conservatively despite the fact that I've watched my diet and still wear the same size I wore in high school.

On the other hand, I don't want to go as anything too stodgy and conservative. Will Danner will be attending the party and I want to make an impression. The right impression. Pepper isn't sure what she wants to be and Eve plans to attend as Eliza Doolittle, the character from *My Fair Lady* and not the singer the girls like to listen to. I've been toying with a character from fiction myself. Finding just the right persona to adequately convey the image I'd like for Will to see has been more vexing than I imagined it would be.

I realize Mr. Danner will most certainly never look at me in quite the same way I look at him, but in spite of what Charlotte thinks, I feel there is no harm in giving my imagination just a bit of free rein. I've never met anyone quite like him. His personality is the perfect blend of archetypes melding the hero, the rebel, and the caregiver. Will is a caring man, a talented teacher, and a lively friend. His real gift, however, seems to be that of a magician because he is more than adept at making an old woman like me feel young again.

Pepper walked up behind me with Morgan in her arms. "Do you need help with Morgan's car seat?"

"It's in the trunk from the last time. I just need to strap it in."

"I'll do it," Pepper offered. "I wouldn't want you to hurt your back."

So much for feeling young.

Later that night, after we'd all returned home, I said my good nights, then headed upstairs for a little one-on-one time with Charlotte. We really had had the best day. We had all managed to find costumes we were happy with and Pepper bought a whole cartful of decorations to spruce up the house. Pepper and Eve were stringing lights around the windows when I decided I'd had enough fun for the day and was ready to come upstairs. Brooklyn had helped in the beginning, until Pi called, and she'd been in her room on the phone ever since.

I like Pi and am happy Brooklyn is interested in him, but I sense he might not return Brooklyn's affection to the same degree. He seems to be more interested in his music than dating, which, I suppose, isn't really all that odd when a young man is just sixteen.

Charlotte curled up on my pillow as I began removing my makeup and moisturizing my skin.

"You should see the costume we got for Morgan," I said to her as she watched me go through the predictable steps of the process. "It's a fuzzy lion that just makes me want to cuddle her up even more than I usually do. It was so cute the way she toddled around the costume shop, growling at everyone. I am finding that I do regret my decision not to have children of my own. I really did miss so much."

Charlotte yawned. It was part of my nightly routine to recount my day to her, but most of the time it appeared as if she wasn't really listening.

"Still, what is done is done and all I can really do is to cherish every minute I have with my adopted family. I am so very excited about Halloween for the first time in my life. Shopping with the girls was so much fun, and Morgan warms my heart every time I'm with her."

I slipped a flannel nightgown over my head and then began sorting the clothes I had removed. I hung those that could be worn again on hangers and separated those that needed laundering into differing baskets for the laundry service.

"We ran into Mr. Danner at the concert," I informed Charlotte as I unwound my bun and began brushing my waist-length hair. "I know we are just friends, and I know that is all we will most likely ever be, but I have to confess the man has a way of making my heart pound and my mood soar."

After I brushed my hair one hundred times I fashioned it into a long braid that hung down my back.

"I know you think I am being a foolish old woman to allow my mind to wander when it comes to thoughts of Will. And I know you are right. But a little fantasy of the romantic kind isn't really all that scandalous." Charlotte jumped off the bed and trotted across the room to the windowsill. She turned her back to me, effectively communicating that she was bored with my chatter.

"I know you tire of hearing about Will but there is no need to be rude."

Charlotte flicked her tail as I straightened the bathroom and headed back into my room.

"Do you think I should ask Will to supper this week? It does seem as if he has enjoyed the meals I have made for him. He still talks about the roast I made that first time he dined with us."

"Meow." Charlotte was still looking out the window. She probably just saw a squirrel and was meowing at it, but I chose to believe she was agreeing with me.

"Yes. That's what I thought as well. It is only neighborly to extend a hand of hospitality to the man. He is after all new to the area, and he hasn't had time to make a lot of friends."

Even as I said this I knew it wasn't true. Will was a friendly man who had made many friends during the short time he has lived in Ashton Falls.

After I was satisfied that I had done everything I needed to do to prepare myself for bed, I set to preparing the room. I worked my way around the area, straightening already perfectly straight books and knickknacks before opening my window just a quarter of an inch.

"Jeremy invited the girls and me to go trick-or-treating with him and Morgan before Zak and Zoe's party on Saturday. I believe he is going with Hank, Madison, and Harper," I said, referring to Zoe's parents and sister. "He said it's a tradition they began last year and would like to continue as the girls get older."

Charlotte tilted her head as she watched me.

"I've been thinking a lot about traditions now that I have the girls in my life. I'd very much like to establish some new ones with them. Costume shopping was a start, and decorating the house has been fun. Zak and Zoe have their big Halloween bash every year, so I suppose attending can become another tradition. I would like something special that is just ours, though."

Charlotte rolled over onto her back. I sat down on the side of the bed and gave her stomach a scratch. I then slid between my 1500-thread count sheets and settled in.

"Are you ready?"

Charlotte indicated she was.

I placed my reading glasses on the tip of my nose, adjusted the light, and opened the book I'd chosen from the bookcase. Charlotte crawled into my lap and began to purr as I began to read aloud. Reading aloud to Charlotte was an activity we both enjoyed immensely, and it was a rare occasion when we missed this ritual at the end of the day. Tonight we were continuing Bram Stoker's *Dracula*. I opened the book to chapter 11.

LUCY WESTENRA'S DIARY

12 September.—How good they all are to me. I quite love that dear Dr. Van Helsing. I wonder why he was so anxious about these flowers. He positively frightened me, he was so fierce. And yet he must have been right, for I feel comfort from them already. Somehow, I do not dread being alone tonight, and I can go to sleep without fear. I shall not mind any flapping outside the window. Oh, the terrible struggle that I have had against sleep so often of late, the pain of sleeplessness, or the pain of the fear of sleep, and with such unknown horrors as it has for me! How blessed are some people, whose lives have no fears, no dreads, to whom sleep is a blessing that comes nightly, and brings nothing but sweet dreams. Well, here I am tonight, hoping for sleep, and lying like Ophelia in the play, with 'virgin crants and maiden strewments.' I never liked garlic before, but tonight it is delightful! There is peace in its smell. I feel sleep coming already. Goodnight, everybody.

I paused and looked at Charlotte. "Perhaps a special Halloween dinner. I'm thinking fondue would be fun. Or maybe a buffet of some sort, where our guests could sample a wide range of offerings. Now that the weather has cooled I've been thinking about digging out the Crock-Pot. Maybe I'll make a soup. I do so love soup in the fall. We could invite Zak and Zoe and their new family, and of course Jeremy and Morgan. Yes, I do believe that will be just the thing."

Reader Portal:

To return to the main story if you are reading chronologically, return to the top of chapter 5 If you are reading as a short story continue on to Chapter 5 of *Zimmerman Academy*.

Chapter 5

Wednesday, October 28

Our First Dinner Party

There are many things I am certain of, and one of those is the fact that I will forever remember the first dinner party the girls and I threw as a newly formed family. I had never before experienced the sense of belonging that can occur when individuals join together to prepare a meal for those they care about. I invited Mr. Danner, as well as Jeremy and Morgan and Zoe and her family. Brooklyn was happy Pi would be attending, and Pepper asked if she might invite her friend Chad. Surprisingly, Eve wanted to invite Dexter Wilkerson, a student at the Academy who is staying with my good friend Nick Benson, who I invited to come as well.

Before the party the girls and I discussed what to make for our guests.

Pepper suggested chili. It seems her mother made chili for Halloween when she was a child. I thought chili sounded like a wonderful idea, but everyone had their own idea of what this chili should look like. Pepper wanted traditional beef with beans, Eve wanted something vegetarian, and Brooklyn preferred chicken to beef. In the end we made three pots of chili, traditional beef and kidney bean, chicken with white beans, and vegetarian black bean. We also made a huge salad, and I picked up three loaves of crusty sourdough bread from the bakery.

"Do you think this is enough broccoli for the veggie tray?" Pepper asked.

We'd decided to serve a selection of sliced cheese and raw fruits and vegetables as an appetizer.

"That's probably enough broccoli, but I'd slice some more carrots," Brooklyn suggested. "Eve has eaten half the ones we sliced earlier."

"I missed lunch," Eve defended herself.

"I washed the grapes when we got home from the market before putting them in the crisper," I informed Eve, who was assembling the fruit tray.

"Why don't you start setting the table?" I asked Pepper. "Let's use the good dishes tonight."

"How many of us will there be?" Pepper asked.

"Let's see. There are the four of us plus Zoe and her family, bringing us up to nine. If you add Jeremy and Morgan that brings us to eleven, Chad makes twelve, and Dex and Dr. Benson and we have fourteen. Oh, and Mr. Danner. We can't forget Mr. Danner."

Pepper and Brooklyn grinned at each other. I know the girls think Will and I have something going on. But we don't. We are just colleagues. Friends with a number of common interests who enjoy spending time together.

The doorbell rang, announcing our first guests, shortly after Pepper and Brooklyn left the room to set the table.

"I'll get it," Pepper yelled.

By the sudden increase in the volume of conversation in the house I was able to infer that Chad had arrived. Chad and Pepper are about as alike as two friends can be. They are both enthusiastic and talkative, with sunny dispositions and smiles that never waver. They are happy and comfortable in any and all social situations, and there isn't a mean bone in their bodies. Both Chad and Pepper are on the cheer squad at the high school, and both freshmen have joined the yearbook staff as well.

Eve and her date, Dex, on the other hand, are about as different as two people can be. Eve is quiet and introverted, with a serious mind and a conservative way about her. She likes literature and classical music and can be found reading during most of her free time. Dex is loud and colorful. He likes to wear wild clothes and his hair color changes from day to day. He enjoys rock and roll and video games during his free time.

"Jeremy is here with Morgan," Pepper informed me as she returned to the kitchen. "Morgan wants to see the kitty. Pepper introduced her to Annabelle, but Morgan seems set on visiting with Charlotte. Is it okay if I take her up to your room so she can say hi?"

"That's perfectly fine."

Annabelle is a small cat Zoe found for Pepper after she expressed interest in having a pet of her own.

"Oh, and Jeremy told me to tell you that he spoke to Zoe a little while ago and they're running late, but only by a few minutes. She had to make a trip to the south shore today and that totally messed up her schedule."

"That's fine. The wonderful thing about chili in a Crock-Pot is that it is ready and waiting whenever you're ready for it. Would you ask Brooklyn to make sure everyone has the beverage of their choice?"

"Yeah, okay." Pepper left the room.

"How did your history project turn out?" I asked Eve, who was preparing the salad.

"Good. The teacher really liked the fact that I took the time to cover both sides of the issue equally. Professor Carlton really had a lot of good input. I'm glad Zak talked him into helping out at the Academy."

"Professor Carlton is a very nice man," I agreed. Ethan is a retired history professor who belongs to the same book club Zoe and I do.

"I asked him if he wanted to come tonight, but I guess he had other plans. Do you think I should add bell pepper to the salad?"

"I think slices on the top would look nice. We have red and yellow peppers as well."

Zoe and her family and Nick and Dex showed up just as Eve was finishing the salad. She went to greet them, leaving me alone in the kitchen with my thoughts for a few minutes as I prepared the oven for the bread. I loved the hustle and bustle of a family, but I had been alone for a long time, so I enjoyed the quiet as well.

I took a deep breath as the scents mingled to create quite a pleasant aroma. In a way, the three young women who I share my life with are like their chili. Each so very different but each complementing the others, so that when combined, they simply work.

"Mind if I come in?" Will Danner poked his head in through the back door.

"Will. What are you doing in the backyard?"

"When I pulled up there were already quite a few cars in the drive, so I parked in the alley. I hope you don't mind."

"Not at all. Come the rest of the way in. I'm almost finished here and then we can join the others."

"Actually, I'm glad we have a few minutes to ourselves."

"You are?" I smiled.

"I've been thinking it might be nice to go to dinner sometime. Just the two of us. Maybe Friday? I know we have Zak and Zoe's party on Saturday."

Was Will asking me out on a date?

"I'd enjoy having dinner with you."

Will let out a breath. Had he been nervous about asking me?

"Did you have something specific in mind?" I asked.

"There's a new steak house on the west shore of the lake. I hear the food is excellent and the view is spectacular. They have live music as well. Perhaps we could throw in a little dancing."

Dancing? As in Will's body pressed close to mine as we moved to the seductive rhythm of a band? I turned my head slightly so he wouldn't notice that my face had most likely turned red.

"You don't like to dance?" Will asked, I'm sure in response to my silence.

"I do. It's just that I'm not really very good at it. I took lessons as a teen, but I haven't had a lot of opportunity to practice since."

"Don't worry. My wife and I used to go dancing all the time. Just follow my lead and you'll be fine."

I smiled again. "Thank you. I'd love to go dancing."

"I'll pick you up at six."

"Six will be fine." I turned to stir the chili, which really didn't need to be stirred. I needed a moment to gather my thoughts. I decided it was best to change the subject. "I'm glad you're planning to attend the party on Saturday. Zoe's parties are always a good time. I even let the girls help me pick out a costume. How about you? Are you dressing up?"

"Actually, I am. I bought a monk's robe from the costume shop when I was in town last week. It is both simple and comfortable."

I laughed. "Perhaps I should go as a nun."

"And cover up all that beautiful hair?"

"I had the best evening," I said to Charlotte as I began my nightly ritual. "Everyone loved the chili buffet. I think the girls and I may have started something. There was even talk of adding a seafood option to the mix for next year's party."

Charlotte sat on the bathroom floor and watched me as I took off my makeup.

"I have to say, I was surprised at the chemistry Eve and Dex seemed to share. I would never in a million years have pegged them as a potential couple. They are as different as night and day and yet together they seem to work."

I applied the first of three moisturizers to my face. My mama had taught me the importance of a religious moisturizing routine and I stick to it to this day.

"And of course Pepper and Chad were as loud and funny as always. I do enjoy their energy. They have a way of lighting up the room and making everyone feel happier. I'm a little worried about Pi and Brooklyn, however."

I began to brush my long, thick hair. One hundred strokes every night keeps it healthy and shiny.

"Brooklyn seems as enamored with Pi as she has been from the first day she met him, but Pi seemed more interested in talking to Jeremy. Of course Pi and Jeremy play in the band together and I know music is important to Pi. And I suppose Pi and Brooklyn are a little young to be in a serious relationship, yet I can see that is what Brooklyn is hoping for. I know her breakup with her last boyfriend was hard on her. I suppose she is ready to move on."

I braided my hair as I always did before going to bed and then began tidying the bathroom.

"Relationships are complicated. I just hope Brooklyn doesn't get her heart broken."

After I was satisfied that I had done everything I needed to do to prepare myself for bed, I set about preparing the room. I worked my way around the area, straightening already perfectly straight books and knickknacks before opening my window just a quarter of an inch.

"Will asked me to dinner on Friday. Although he wasn't specific, I got the feeling he was asking me on a real date. We are even going dancing. I have to admit the thought of dancing with Will brings butterflies to my stomach. It's been so long since I've enjoyed a man's embrace as we sway to the music. I wonder what I should wear."

Charlotte began swatting at the decorative pillows I have stacked on my bed. It was obvious she wanted me to move things along.

"I suppose I'll ask for input from the girls. They are always so good about knowing which clothes best fit each social situation."

After stacking the extra pillows on my white tufted chaise I poured myself a cup of tea from the warming pot I'd already brought up and added a splash of brandy. Then I slid between my 1500-thread count sheets and settled in.

I reached up and touched the end of my long braid. "Mr. Danner said I had beautiful hair."

I sighed as I remembered the thrill of his smile.

After placing my reading glasses on the tip of my nose, I adjusted the light and opened the book we were reading. Charlotte crawled into my lap and began to purr as I began to read *Dracula* aloud. Tonight we would start with chapter 16 of Bram Stoker's masterpiece.

DR. SEWARD'S DIARY-cont.

It was just a quarter before twelve o'clock when we got into the churchyard over the low wall. The night was dark with occasional gleams of moonlight between the dents of the heavy clouds that scudded across the sky. We all kept somehow close together, with Van Helsing slightly in front as he led the way. When we had come close to the tomb I looked well at Arthur, for I feared the proximity to a place laden with so sorrowful a memory would upset him, but he bore himself well. I took it that the very mystery of the proceeding was in some way a counteractant to his grief. The Professor unlocked the door, and seeing a natural hesitation amongst us for various reasons, solved the difficulty by entering first himself. The rest of us followed, and he closed the door. He then lit a dark lantern and pointed to a coffin. Arthur stepped forward hesitatingly. Van Helsing said to me, "You were with me here yesterday. Was the body of Miss Lucy in that coffin?"

"It was."

The Professor turned to the rest saying, "You hear, and yet there is no one who does not believe with me."

He took his screwdriver and again took off the lid of the coffin. Arthur looked on, very pale but silent. When the lid was removed he stepped forward. He evidently did not know that there was a leaden coffin, or at any rate, had not thought of it. When he saw the rent in the lead, the blood rushed to his face for an instant, but as quickly fell away again, so that he remained of a ghastly whiteness. He was still silent. Van Helsing forced back the leaden flange, and we all looked in and recoiled.

The coffin was empty!

"Oh, my." I cuddled with Charlotte. "I'm glad I have you to keep me company tonight. It seems that tales from the crypt are best read during the day."

Charlotte began to purr. Obviously, stories about empty coffins didn't bother her in the least. I continued to scratch Charlotte behind the ears as I read. Eventually, it was the steady rhythm of her purr and not the book that lulled me into a deep and dreamless sleep.

Reader Portal:

To return to the main story if you are reading the story chronologically, return to the top of chapter 14. If you are reading as a short story continue on to Chapter 6 of *Zimmerman Academy*.

Chapter 6

Friday, October 30

I will always remember the first real date Will and I shared. My heart pounded right through my chest as he drove me home from our evening together. It had been a magical night I knew I would never forget. The food had been delicious, the music romantic, and the setting enchanting. Will had been funny and entertaining as he told me stories about his life up to that point, and I could feel myself falling in love just a little bit more with each memory he shared. I remember the way my heart stopped beating when we pulled up in front of the house. I'd worried and fantasized since he'd asked me out whether this meal together would end with a kiss.

"I had a lovely time," I stammered.

I could see a movement behind the curtains, so I knew the girls were watching. They'd been so sweet as they'd helped me to prepare for my date earlier in the day. I think in some ways they'd been as nervous as I was.

"I enjoyed myself too," Will replied.

He put the car into park, turned off the ignition, and turned to look at me. He seemed as nervous as I, which was ridiculous considering the man had been married for thirty years and so had logically shared many kisses.

"It seems we have an audience." Will laughed as he nodded toward the house.

I turned and looked at the three faces staring down on us from an upstairs window.

"Yes." I blushed. "The girls were excited that we were going out. I'm sure they waited to hear all about it."

Will took my hand in his and leaned in just a bit. "I'm happy the girls look out for you the way they do. It's a testament to the fine woman you are. But I'd sort of like our first time to be without an audience."

"First time?" I whispered. I felt my body begin to shake, although it wasn't cold in the car in the least.

Will closed the distance between us and gently touched his lips with mine. I closed my eyes as my entire body exploded in a longing I had never before experienced.

Will leaned back just a bit and smiled. He looked at me and his grin grew bigger. "Breathe," he suggested.

I let out the breath I'd been holding. I wanted to be embarrassed that I'd acted like such a fool, totally forgetting to breathe after such an innocent kiss, but Will leaned in and kissed me again, longer and harder, before I could think about it too much.

"Would you like to go out again?" Will asked. "Perhaps a picnic on Sunday?"

"I would," I whispered.

"Good." Will smiled in such a way as to light up his face. "Around noon?"

"Noon would be perfect."

Will looked toward the house again. The girls were still watching from the window. "I guess you should go in. I'm afraid they'll come out after you if you don't."

"Yes," I agreed. "They do tend to be a bit protective."

Suddenly, it hit me that Brooklyn, Eve, and Pepper were the only people in the world to have worried about me since my parents when I was a child. The thought of having people who cared about my daily movements after all these years made my heart feel full and grateful.

Will came around and opened the door for me. He took my hand in his as we walked up the walkway to the front door. I loved the way his large hand felt as it covered my much smaller one. The man was tall and fit and I felt like a schoolgirl as I imagined his wonderfully perfect hands on my body. He paused as we reached the front porch. He turned and pulled me into his embrace.

"This one is for them." He laughed as his mouth met mine briefly one final time before he opened the door and ushered me inside.

"Stop that," I scolded Charlotte as she swatted at my feet while I prepared for bed later that evening.

"Meow."

I stopped what I was doing and looked down. "I suppose I haven't maintained my side of the conversation this evening. It's just that the night was so incredibly perfect that I am afraid if I speak it will break the spell."

Charlotte tilted her head as she listened to what I was saying.

"I know it's silly, but I almost feel as if the night was a dream and the only way to maintain the dream is to be perfectly still, perfectly silent."

I straightened the room after I had moisturized and prepared for bed. I took in a deep breath of the crisp autumn air as I opened the window just an inch. As I began to sort the decorative pillows I kept on my bed, Charlotte jumped up onto the thick winter comforter and knocked the book we have been reading to the floor.

"Yes, I will read to you tonight. I always do. I believe we can finish the book. And just in time for Halloween."

After placing my reading glasses on the tip of my nose, I adjusted the light and opened the book we were reading. Charlotte crawled into my lap and began to purr as I began to read Bram Stoker's *Dracula* aloud. Tonight we would continue with chapter 25.

I think that none of us were surprised when we were asked to see Mrs. Harker a little before the time of sunset. We have of late come to understand that sunrise and sunset are to her times of peculiar freedom. When her old self can be manifest without any controlling force subduing or restraining her, or inciting her to action. This mood or condition begins some half hour or more before actual sunrise or sunset, and lasts till either the sun is high, or whilst the clouds are still aglow with the rays streaming above the horizon. At first there is a sort of negative condition, as if some tie were loosened, and then the absolute freedom quickly follows. When, however, the freedom ceases the change back or relapse comes quickly, preceded only by a spell of warning silence.

I realized Charlotte and I had already read this passage, so I skimmed down the page to the point where we'd left off. Charlotte didn't care if we reread the same passages, but I found that this evening I was anxious to finish so that I could be alone with my thoughts.

"That I may die now, either by my own hand or that of another, before the greater evil is entirely wrought. I know, and you know, that were I once dead you could and would set free my immortal spirit, even as you did my poor Lucy's. Were death, or the fear of death, the only thing that stood in the way I would not shrink to die here now, amidst the friends who love me. But death is not all. I cannot believe that to die in such a case, when there is hope before us and a bitter task to be done, is God's will. Therefore, I on my part, give up here the certainty of eternal

rest, and go out into the dark where may be the blackest things that the world or the nether world holds!"

We were all silent, for we knew instinctively that this was only a prelude. The faces of the others were set, and Harker's grew ashen grey. Perhaps, he guessed better than any of us what was coming.

I paused and looked at Charlotte. I had to wonder if my date was but a prelude to things to come. And although the book predicted darkness, I hoped my own story would be magical and endearing.

Reader Portal:

To return to the main story if you are reading the story chronologically, return to the top of chapter 14. If you are reading as a short story you are done. I hope you enjoyed it.

SANTA SLEUTH

A ZOE DONOVAN MYSTERY

WITH RECIPES

BY KATHI DALEY

http://www.amazon.com/Santa-Sleuth-Donovan-Mystery-Book-ebook/dp/B015EXE6I4/ref=sr_1_1?s=digital-text&ie=UTF8&qid=1442440956&sr=1-1&keywords=santa+sleuth

Recipes for Ghostly Graveyard

Recipes by Kathi

Easy Beefy Chili
White Bean Chili
Easy Vegetarian Black Bean Chili

Recipes by Readers

Aunt Lena's Candied Corn – submitted by Connie Correll
Pumpkin Dip – submitted by Marie Rice
Popcorn Cake – submitted by Brandy Barber
Graveyard Dirt – submitted by Nancy Farris
Great Halloween Fun Fondue Dinner – submitted by
Shirley Ericson
Bacon Macaroni and Cheese Supreme – submitted by
Joanne Kocourek

Easy Beefy Chili

This recipe is really just a doctoring of a canned offering, but the end result is delish! I make it almost every Halloween so we can warm our insides before we travel outdoors for trick-or-treating.

Brown 1 pound of ground beef; I use extra lean.

Season with Lawry's salt, garlic powder, pepper, chili powder, and cayenne pepper—I haven't put quantities because this is really personal preference; I like my chili spicy, so I add a lot of cayenne pepper and chili powder.

Add 1 or 2 large cans of chili with beans; I prefer Nalley, but any brand is fine. If the mixture seems too thick—and it might—thin it with a little water or broth.

Let the chili simmer for a bit so the flavors from the canned chili can meld with the flavors of the seasoned beef.

Meanwhile:
Fry a pound of bacon until crispy and crumble into bacon bits.
Grate a desired amount of cheddar cheese; I use extra sharp.
Dice an onion.
Spoon sour cream into a serving bowl.
When you're ready to serve let each person garnish their chili as desired.

Serve with warm tortilla chips.

White Bean Chili

4 chicken breasts, cubed
Sauté in olive oil until chicken is cooked through.

Add:
1 onion, diced
2 carrots, diced
2 stalks celery, diced
2 cloves garlic, diced

Sauté until veggies are tender.

Add to chicken mixture:
2 cans Great Northern White Beans
1 can chicken broth
2 cans diced Ortega Green Chiles
1 tsp. salt
1 tsp. cumin
1 tsp. oregano
1 tsp. pepper
1 tsp. cayenne pepper (or more if you like it hot)

Cook over medium heat until warm.

Stir in:
1 cup sour cream
½ cup heavy whipping cream

Heat for a few more minutes.
Serve with tortillas.

Easy Vegetarian Black Bean Chili

Sauté in small amount of olive oil:

1 bell pepper, diced
1 onion, diced
2 cloves garlic, chopped

Add:

1 tsp. cumin
1 tsp. oregano
2 tsp. chili powder

Add:

1 tub salsa (I use hot, but you can use mild)
1 15-oz. can black beans, drained

Cook on medium heat until warm.

Serve with rice and tortillas.

Aunt Lena's Candied Popcorn

Submitted by Connie Correll

This is a traditional favorite for the holidays from my Aunt Lena.

5 qt. popped corn
¾ cup white Karo Syrup
¼ lb. margarine
2 tbs. water
1 lb. powdered sugar
1 cup miniature marshmallows

Stir all of the above in a 5-qt. pan *except* corn and heat at a low temperature until it *just* comes to a boil. Stir constantly so as not to burn the mixture. Pour over the popped corn and toss to coat.

Pumpkin Dip

Submitted by Marie Rice

This tastes like the filling of a pumpkin pie without your having to do all that cooking or pastry rolling. Yum!

1 pkg. (8 oz.) cream cheese, softened
1 can (15 oz.) pumpkin
½ cup brown sugar
1 tbs. pumpkin pie spice

In a large mixing bowl beat cream cheese, pumpkin, and sugar until smooth. (It might actually have a few little lumps in it; that's fine.) Add the spices and beat until smooth.

Refrigerate to chill.

Makes approx. 3 cups.

Serve with apple slices, graham crackers, graham sticks, gingersnaps, or any little "dipper" you can think of. My personal favorite dippers with this recipe are gingersnap cookies and slices of Granny Smith apples. And sometimes I just grab a spoon and eat it right out of the bowl!

Popcorn Cake

Submitted by Brandy Barber

This was one of my favorite things my Grandma Marsh would fix when we all got together.

½ cup corn oil
½ cup butter
1 lb. marshmallows
16 cups popped popcorn (take out unpopped kernels)
½ lb. peanuts
1 lb. M&M's (you can pick different colors and kinds for the holidays)

Put oil, butter, and marshmallows in pan and heat. Blend well. Pour over popcorn and nuts; mix halfway. Add M&M's and mix well. Press into buttered angel food pan (I have also used a Bundt cake pan lined with wax paper). Refrigerate until hard.

Graveyard Dirt

Submitted by Nancy Farris

For Halloween I make this into a graveyard. For summer picnics, I use vanilla Oreos and put them in a sand pail and use the sand scoop as the serving spoon.

½ stick butter
8 oz. cream cheese
1 cup sugar
2 small pkgs. instant vanilla pudding
3 cups milk
12 oz. Cool Whip
1 bag Oreo cookies

Cream butter, cream cheese, and sugar together until smooth.

Separately mix pudding, milk, and Cool Whip.
Fold in the cream cheese mixture.

Run the Oreos through the chopper of a food processor or blender for the dirt (use the entire cookie).

In a 9 x 13 dish, layer pudding mix, then dirt and pudding and dirt with dirt on top, and then garnish with gummy worms and marshmallow ghosts, etc. I also use cookies as tombstones!

Great Halloween Fun Fondue Dinner

Submitted by Shirley Ericson

2 cups olive oil
1 lb. butter
2 flowers fresh garlic, all cloves pressed
4 cans anchovies
Sliced French bread
Fondue forks

Sauce:
Place all ingredients in electric fry pan on low until anchovies mix into sauce.

Prepare the following to fondue:
Every kind of fresh vegetables in bite-size pieces, e.g., mushrooms, broccoli, zucchini, Brussels sprouts (cut in half), green beans, etc.
Prepare fresh sirloin steak, chicken, shrimp, etc., into bite-size pieces.

Each person takes fresh vegetables and meat on plate and sautés all in the sauce; watch for degree desired.

Pour over French bread.

Serve with wine. You will want to go back for more.

Bacon Macaroni and Cheese Supreme

Submitted by Joanne Kocourek

Macaroni and cheese is one of my family's favorite comfort foods with creamy, stringy, cheesy goodness. I wanted to provide something special, better than packaged mac and cheese. It's extremely easy to individualize the special ingredients and servings in small ramekins as a special treat. Mac and cheese is always better when crisp bacon goodness is involved, especially in this easy, no-fuss 30-minute dish from start to finish!

Ingredients:
8 oz. elbow macaroni or cavatappi pasta
8 slices bacon, diced
2½ cups heavy cream (or whipping cream if heavy cream isn't available)
2 cloves garlic, minced
1 tbs. fresh thyme leaves, chopped
⅓ cup shallots, minced
1 tsp. Dijon mustard
1¼ cups shredded Gruyère cheese or smoked Gruyère
¼ cup grated Parmesan
½ cup shredded Cheddar cheese (reserve for topping)
Kosher salt and freshly ground black pepper, to taste

1 small can chunky lobster or salmon, drained, warmed in microwave (optional)

In large pot of boiling salted water, cook pasta according to package instructions; drain well and set aside.

Heat a large skillet over medium-high heat. Add bacon and cook until brown and crispy, about 6–8 minutes. Transfer to a paper towel–lined plate. Reserve 4 tsp. of crisp bacon for garnish.

In a medium saucepan, combine heavy cream, garlic, thyme, shallots, and mustard over medium heat. Bring to a slight boil and reduce by half, about 4–5 minutes. Stir in cheeses, a handful at a time, until smooth, about 1–2 minutes; season with salt and pepper to taste. Stir in pasta and bacon until well combined.

Divide the pasta mix into 4 ramekins.

Add special optional ingredients if desired and stir gently to mix

Top each with shredded Cheddar cheese and reserved crisp bacon. Broil 2–3 minutes if desired.
Serve immediately.

Note: By dividing the servings into individual ramekins, you can add lobster or salmon to the individual servings prior to broiling for those who appreciate lobster or seafood mac and cheese.

Books by Kathi Daley

Come for the murder, stay for the romance.
Buy them on Amazon today.

Zoe Donovan Cozy Mystery:

Halloween Hijinks
The Trouble With Turkeys
Christmas Crazy
Cupid's Curse
Big Bunny Bump-off
Beach Blanket Barbie
Maui Madness
Derby Divas
Haunted Hamlet
Turkeys, Tuxes, and Tabbies
Christmas Cozy
Alaskan Alliance
Matrimony Meltdown
Soul Surrender
Heavenly Honeymoon
Hopscotch Homicide
Ghostly Graveyard
Santa Sleuth – *December 2015*

Paradise Lake Cozy Mystery:
Pumpkins in Paradise
Snowmen in Paradise
Bikinis in Paradise
Christmas in Paradise
Puppies in Paradise
Halloween in Paradise

Whales and Tails Cozy Mystery:
Romeow and Juliet
The Mad Catter
Grimm's Furry Tail
Much Ado About Felines
Legend of Tabby Hollow
Cat of Christmas Past – *November 2015*

Seacliff High Mystery:
The Secret
The Curse
The Relic
The Conspiracy
The Grudge – *December 2015*

Road to Christmas Romance:
Road to Christmas Past

Kathi Daley lives with her husband, kids, grandkids, and Bernese mountain dogs in beautiful Lake Tahoe. When she isn't writing, she likes to read (preferably at the beach or by the fire), cook (preferably something with chocolate or cheese), and garden (planting and planning, not weeding). She also enjoys spending time on the water when she's not hiking, biking, or snowshoeing the miles of desolate trails surrounding her home.

Kathi uses the mountain setting in which she lives, along with the animals (wild and domestic) that share her home, as inspiration for her cozy mysteries.

Stay up-to-date with her newsletter, *The Daley Weekly*. There's a link to sign up on both her Facebook page and her website, or you can access the sign-in sheet at:
 http://eepurl.com/NRPDf

Visit Kathi:

Facebook at Kathi Daley Books,
www.facebook.com/kathidaleybooks

Kathi Daley Teen –
www.facebook.com/kathidaleyteen

Kathi Daley Books Group Page –
https://www.facebook.com/groups/569578823146850/

Kathi Daley Books Birthday Club- get a book on your birthday - https://www.facebook.com/groups/1040638412628912/

Kathi Daley Recipe Exchange - https://www.facebook.com/groups/752806778126428/

Webpage - www.kathidaley.com

E-mail - kathidaley@kathidaley.com

Recipe Submission E-mail – kathidaleyrecipes@kathidaley.com

Goodreads: https://www.goodreads.com/author/show/7278377.Kathi_Daley

Twitter at Kathi Daley@kathidaley - https://twitter.com/kathidaley

Tumblr - http://kathidaleybooks.tumblr.com/

Amazon Author Page - http://www.amazon.com/Kathi-Daley/e/B00F3BOX4K/ref=sr_tc_2_0?qid=1418237358&sr=8-2-ent

Pinterest - http://www.pinterest.com/kathidaley/

45542873R00154

Made in the USA
Lexington, KY
01 October 2015